Psalms 121:1,2
Because He lives,
Lizann Baker
2016

LESSONS *of*
HONOR

BY LIZANN BAKER

Copyright © 2015 by LizAnn Baker

Lessons of Honor
by LizAnn Baker

Printed in the United States of America.

ISBN 9781498449182

All rights reserved solely by the author. The author guarantees all contents are original and do not infringe upon the legal rights of any other person or work. No part of this book may be reproduced in any form without the permission of the author. The views expressed in this book are not necessarily those of the publisher.

Unless otherwise indicated, Scripture quotations taken from the King James Version (KJV) – public domain

Photograph used by permission from Goodrich Photography.

www.xulonpress.com

SUMMARY: LESSONS OF HONOR

Lessons of Honor is the story of Sara, a diminutive young teen who is orphaned, and becomes an indentured servant to a family that has no love for her. As she serves the Haley family, she looks to God to deliver her and protect her. She struggles with the only son, Judson Haley, who becomes enamored with her as she approaches her eighteenth birthday. After suffering an attack by him, Sara escapes her tormentor and stays one step ahead of him as she goes west.

As Sara continues to flee her pursuer, she meets friends along the way that help her escape detection. Without warning, she finds herself in a life and death situation. Rescued by a much older man, she finds safety and peace for the first time. She marries him in hopes of continued safety and to give her unborn child a name. Soon after she marries, she faces more heartache. She then meets the true love of her life. Sara has to decide what she will do to resolve her problems with Jud, the man she marries, and the man she loves.

Lessons of Honor reflects on marriage vows and their importance in the decisions we make in our lives. Sara learns the value of prayer as it is the lifeline in her life. As her faith grows, she becomes more and more willing to let God work in her life even when there seems no possibility of hope as she learns about honor and the price she must pay for it.

DEDICATION

The other day I read that if we have the ability to create something, like a story or painting or invention, it is because we are made in the image of God. God is the Creator of the heavens, the earth and everything in them. So the ability to create comes as a gift from Him. I can think of no one better to give praise and dedication to for helping me create this book than my Lord, Yeshua.

CHAPTER ONE

SARA

Sara stood looking at the sunset behind the house. She could only spare a few moments before she would be missed, and that could lead to trouble for her. Sara looked up to see the sky above her. It was clear with only a few clouds on the western horizon reflecting a red glow. Red sky at night, sailor's delight, she thought to herself. She was no sailor, and tomorrow looked like more storms to her.

It seemed impossible that two and a half years ago, she was with her father in another town, keeping house and knowing what it meant to be loved. Then he'd been thrown by a horse and landed on a rock. After being in a coma for a few days, he stopped breathing and Sara was alone – all alone. Everything her father owned was sold to pay his debts. The question was what to do with Sara. She was only thirteen at the time. Her mother had died of influenza the winter after her father had returned from the Civil War when Sara was only eight, and there had only been her father and herself left. Now he was gone. It seemed the God her father loved had abandoned him and Sara.

Sara turned to go back into the kitchen and finish cleaning up the supper things. The courts had decided she should be apprenticed out to a family to learn how to care for a house. It was as though she didn't already know how after keeping house for her father for five years. Here she was at the Haley farm. She had spent four and a half years at Mrs. Haley's beck and call, treated more as a slave. Mr. Haley was a silent man, who seldom spoke and let Mrs. Haley have her way in everything but the farming. As far as he was concerned, Sara didn't even exist. She slept in the back storeroom that was hot in the summer and without heat in the winter. She cooked, cleaned, washed clothes, and tended the garden and canning, as well as anything else that came to Mrs. Haley's mind. She had often felt the back hand of the missus when Sara moved too slowly or something was not to her liking.

Through it all Sara continued to trust in the Lord. She often thought about Joseph of the Bible and what he went through with his brothers when he was sold as a slave, and how God had used all the bad things in his life for his good and that of his family. Sara decided that if Joseph could stand firm in his faith through slavery and imprisonment, she could stand firm in her faith in this situation, except for one problem. Living with the Haley family would be tolerable, if it wasn't for the son, Judson Haley.

When she first came to the Haley farm, Jud simply ignored the skinny, silent girl. Jud was a shiftless, lazy, no account of a son. He was a tall strapping young man with a sullen look about him. His straw-colored hair always needed trimmed. His eyes were blue, but beady. He constantly had a smirk on his face as though life was simply a joke. He said and did the right things whenever he had an audience, especially his parents. His mother thought the world of him and could find no fault with anything he did.

Things had changed over time. Sara was barely an inch over five feet and was small framed. Her brown hair was dark, and matched her oversized brown eyes which seemed to dominate her face. Her lips were full, especially when she pouted. Her light complexion, which burned easily in the sun, fit the rosy cheeks she had which blushed so easily. Jud was no longer a teenager as he had recently turned twenty. Sara was fast becoming an attractive young woman, and that had caught Jud's eye. He was always trying to corner her or grab at her. He made vulgar comments under his breath when he passed her, and Sara was very careful not to be caught alone with him. He could do no wrong in his parents' eyes, and if Sara had a problem, she brought it on herself with her proud ways, according to the missus.

LESSONS OF HONOR

Life was never easy before, but now it was becoming intolerable for Sara.

Sara finished her chores in the kitchen and headed back to the storeroom to work on her crocheted collars. She had been taught by her mother as a young girl how to do the fancy crochet stitches used in collars for ladies' finery. Every spare minute she could find, she worked on the collars. Whenever Mrs. Haley needed to go to town, she took Sara with her and always sent her to do the shopping at the main store for groceries and sundry other items. Heaven forbid that Mrs. Haley would be seen in such a store. She usually went to the millinery shop or the dress shop.

Sara didn't mind doing the shopping. She had made friends with the shopkeeper and arranged with him to sell her collars in his store. He kept a portion of each sale and she got the rest. She saved every penny she earned as a nest egg. The Haley's paid her nothing for her work. They claimed she got free room and board as well as clothes and a good upbringing from them. The truth was, she had one dress that was a hand me down from Mrs. Haley, and one skirt and two blouses for every day. Sara knew one day, she would need money in order to leave this place. The Haley's knew nothing about her business arrangement or the secret stash she had hidden away in the storeroom.

Sara worked on the collars until the house had been quiet for a half an hour or more. She didn't dare lay down for the night until the rest of the household was in bed asleep, for she now lived in fear that Jud might come to the storeroom. There was no lock on the door, but Sara managed to prop it shut with a barrel to delay quick access and give her warning of his approach. Still she stayed fully clothed until the house became quiet, then she could let her guard down for a few short hours.

Sara was now seventeen and would turn eighteen in a few more weeks. Though she sometimes felt God had abandoned her, she still prayed daily for His hand in her life. She wanted those things she no longer had, like respect and dignity. She would even be willing to forego love if she could be with someone who would honor and care about her and respect her wishes. But that wasn't going to happen at the Haley farm, and never with Jud Haley there.

Sara finally put her handwork away and got ready for bed. She closed her eyes in prayer. Sara believed God could turn everything that happened to her into good for her life. Her father had believed that and taught her to do the same. She knew that God was her only hope, and she refused to give up her trust in Him. As she rested on her cot, she tried to remember that God was in charge of her life. She had been twelve when she asked the Lord Jesus to come into her heart. She was all alone now, but she knew her father always said the Lord was the only One you could trust and depend on to guide you in life. She had asked the Lord to help her. He was the One who had kept her going when her father died. He was the One she turned to now. Still deep inside of her, she had a growing fear of Jud. She tried to turn that fear over to God as there was nothing else she could do about it. Sara sighed and closed her eyes. Eventually sleep found her.

CHAPTER TWO

BIRTHDAY

"Sara, I expect everything to go perfectly. The ladies coming today are used to the finest and I expect them to see that the Haley's do, too. Is everything ready for the tea?"

"Yes, Mrs. Haley. The tea things are ready to go. I have done everything you asked and the food is ready as well."

"I expect you to be seen and not heard unless you are directly spoken to by one of the ladies. Remember to address me properly. When you are not needed, I expect you to stay in the kitchen and listen for the bell. Is that dress the best you have?"

"Yes, ma'am."

"Well, at least the apron is clean. I think I hear a carriage now. Answer the door and direct the ladies into the parlor. I'll be waiting there. Lay their things on the couch in the office and be very careful with them. Don't get anyone's things mixed up. Now, go to the front door." With that, Mrs. Haley left for the parlor in a swish of her skirt and click of her shoes.

Sara headed for the door. Soon a tap was heard and she ushered in Mrs. Appleton and led her into the parlor and carried her things into the office. Another knock and two more ladies entered. Within twenty minutes, all five guests had been shown to the parlor and were busy talking, while Sara laid their things in the office, carefully keeping everything neat until their return.

Sara headed for the kitchen. She set the tea kettle on to boil so the water would be hot. Everything else was ready as well. Sara sat down with a sigh. She had been working day and night to have everything ready for Mrs. Haley's guests today. She had scrubbed floors and polished furniture, baked special delicacies, starched curtains and ironed them, and still made sure she had supper things for the men ready to go as well. Sara would be glad when this day was over.

The back porch door squeaked as she heard footsteps. Jud entered the kitchen grinning at her like the fool he was.

"Sara," he drawled. "Fancy meeting you here."

"What do you want, Jud?" asked Sara.

"You know what I want." Jud smiled and stepped nearer. "I just had to get something out of the office, and thought I might get a little *treat* on my way through to the office."

"Stay away from me, Jud," said Sara as she stepped back. "You know your mother has a houseful of guests."

"Yes, indeed I do." Again Jud grinned and took another step closer. "I guess that we'd better be real quiet."

The bell tinkled and Sara was glad to escape to the parlor.

Mrs. Haley was reigning over the group like a queen. When Sara entered the doorway, Mrs. Haley barely glanced her way. "Sara, we would like to have our tea served now. Will you please see to it?"

Sara answered, "Yes, ma'am." She turned and started down the hall. To her horror she saw muddy footprints on the floor. Jud had gone into the office and back out, leaving a muddy trail as he went. Sara had only a few minutes to clean it up before serving the tea. At least the tea things were ready. Hastily, she grabbed a bucket and rag and quickly mopped up the footprints. By the time she reached the office door, the prints had faded leaving little evidence of the mud. At least she didn't have the office floor to clean. Sara quickly hurried back into the kitchen and put things away. When she turned to get the tea things, she realized Jud had helped himself to some of the food as he headed out the door. Sara quickly replenished the trays and poured the hot water into the teapot.

She knew Jud had done everything on purpose to make more work for her or to get her in trouble. He never passed up a chance to make her look bad or inept at her work. Of course, his mother believed Jud would never do anything like that, so Sara knew it would do no good to complain about it.

Sara served the tea, and everything else seemed to go well. Mrs. Haley kept Sara running back and forth to the kitchen for things, but all in all, she was able to get it done and cleared the tea things away without any other mishaps. As she worked in the kitchen washing the tea things, the bell sounded once more. Sara quickly dried her hands and headed back to the parlor.

"Sara, would you please get the wraps and bonnets for the ladies?" asked Mrs. Haley as sweetly as possible.

"Yes, ma'am," Sara hurried into the office, but stopped in her tracks at the doorway. Everything was in a muddled heap on the floor. Jud! Sara quickly began to pick up the various wraps and bonnets, but everything was wrinkled or crushed. Sara tried to smooth things out as she picked them up. She desperately tried to remember who wore what as she sorted them out. Just as she was picking up the last item from the floor, Mrs. Haley walked in the room.

"Sara! What is taking so long? The ladies are ready to go! What in the world? What have you done? How dare you treat their things like this!"

"Is there a problem, Edith?" asked Mrs. Appleton who had suddenly arrived at the office door.

BIRTHDAY

"Caroline, I must apologize. I'm afraid Sara is not used to handling the fineries of a lady, and has consequently mistreated your wraps. I will gladly do whatever I can to make things right," gushed Mrs. Haley.

"Well! I guess it is hard to find adequate help so far west of civilization. A few wrinkles can be taken care of, but a crushed hat. That's a different matter. It will have to be replaced, I'm afraid."

"Of course, send me the bill and it will be covered," promised Mrs. Haley.

By that point, the other ladies had come for their things and Mrs. Haley apologized and placated them as graciously as she could. She never lost her poise or her temper until the last lady was waved off in her buggy and left.

Sara made a hasty retreat to the kitchen and continued washing and drying the tea things as well as getting the table set for supper. She knew a storm was headed her way and she quickly prayed for the strength to endure. She heard Mrs. Haley's footsteps in the hallway.

"Sara Morrow. I have never been so humiliated in my life! You did that on purpose and you will pay for what you have done. Right now, I don't want to even see your face! Go to your room and don't come out until tomorrow. I will have to speak to Mr. Haley about this. I don't know if I can ever live this down. These ladies may never speak to me again. Now go!"

Sara left for the storeroom. There she sat utterly dejected. *Why, Lord? Why did Jud have to make her life so miserable? Lord, are you there?* What would happen now? Sara found her sewing basket and started crocheting. She might as well make good use of the extra time. Somehow, she felt she was going to need all the money she could earn. Tears started running down her face as she worked. She heard voices from the kitchen as the men came in for supper. She could hear Jud laughing and felt he was enjoying the trouble he had caused her. She could also hear Mrs. Haley's voice raised in pitch and anger and knew that everything that had happened was being reviewed and she was coming up as the culprit.

As another tear slid down her cheek, Sara remembered the day. This was her birthday. She turned eighteen today and no one knew. Happy Birthday, Sara, she thought, Happy Birthday.

CHAPTER THREE
PUNISHMENT

The next morning Sara was up early and had breakfast well under way when Mrs. Haley came into the kitchen. She stood at the doorway and took in the set table, bacon browning in the pan, coffee hot on the stove and the smell of biscuits baking. She cleared her voice and Sara looked at her.

"Sara, your behavior yesterday was simply unacceptable."

"But Mrs. Haley, I wasn't the one . . ."

"Quiet! I'll not hear any lies you have made up to excuse yourself. I have tried to treat you as a relative and provide a home for you, but I feel you have simply thrown my benevolence back into my face. You are soon going to be eighteen and your apprenticeship will end. I had hoped you might remain here and even become a permanent part of our household, but you've proven you are not fit to stay. I'll expect you to be gone by the end of the summer. I'm sorry, but I will not be able in good conscience to give you any letter of recommendation. I will try to give you chores to do that will keep you busy outside and not in the house, except for laundry and ironing. They and the cooking will keep you in the kitchen. I do not want you in any other part of the house, except the storeroom." Mrs. Haley turned and walked out of the kitchen.

Sara knew it would do her no good to tell Mrs. Haley what had happened. She knew that down deep inside she would be glad to go. If Mrs. Haley was truthful, she would also admit that she wanted to keep Sara around to do the hard work, especially the canning before the summer ended. But then where would Sara go? No one around this area would hire her if Mrs. Haley had anything to do with it.

Sara turned back and checked the biscuits. They were almost done. I should just walk out and let them burn, she thought. What good would that do? She stiffened her back. She wasn't going to let Jud get to her. She started to crack eggs to fry.

Sara began to plan what she would do. She had a little money from the crocheted collars she had been able to sell. She didn't have much to pack, so she definitely would be traveling light, but to where? What would she do when she got there? She supposed she could look for work as a cook or a maid if there were someone willing to hire a girl as young as she was.

Lord, You are going to have to lead me. Show me what You would have me do and where I should go. I don't even know if I should go east or west. Direct me as I try to make plans.

Breakfast was soon ready and everyone was seated at the table. Jud had his usual grin on his face. Sara tried to ignore him and kept her eyes on her plate. She quickly ate and then excused herself. She went out to hoe in the garden. It wasn't long before she heard someone walking up behind her. She turned, holding the hoe in a defensive way.

"Whoa now, Sara, you look like you want to use that hoe on me," laughed Jud.

"Why not? After all the trouble you caused yesterday, you need to be taken down a peg or two." Sara stared at him angrily.

Jud stepped closer to her and grabbed the end of the hoe. "This hoe couldn't stop me, Missy. I would treat you real fine if'n you'd come down off your high horse and show me a little respect." Jud leered at her.

"There's nothing I can see to respect!" Sara spat the words out.

"Listen, Missy, there's coming a day very soon when I'm going to teach you a thing or two. Just you wait. I'll teach you a lesson, that's for sure. I want you, Sara, and I'll have you or no one will. You'll be sorry one day for your high-handed ways. You'll be mine, have no doubt about that." Jud shoved the hoe at her and abruptly turned and stomped off.

Sara discovered her heart was pounding. "Never in a lifetime, Jud. I will have nothing to do with the likes of you! I'll go so far from here, you'll never find me!" Sara blurted the words out to his retreating back.

Jud stopped in his tracks and quietly turned and took a few steps back toward Sara. "You could never run far enough that I wouldn't find you. No matter where you might hide, I'd find you. I will have you, Sara, on that you can be sure." The look in his eyes bore through her, and then he turned walking away again.

Jud scared her down deep. She was afraid of him and his threats. She would need to be more careful than ever and not let Jud catch her somewhere alone. *Lord, help me*, she silently prayed. She turned and went back to hoeing.

Every day now, Mrs. Haley was constantly watching Sara. She gave her all the hardest and dirtiest chores to do. She never gave Sara a chance to rest, but kept her working all the day long. If Sara wasn't quick enough, she would scold her and call her names. If Sara dared to say anything, she would be slapped for back-talking. With each passing day, Sara was becoming more and more discouraged. When Mrs. Haley announced that she was going to town the next day, she informed Sara she could not come, but must stay and work on the laundry and ironing.

Sara found herself looking forward to being free from under Mrs. Haley's thumb. She might have to work all day, but at least she could do it peacefully without having the missus looking over her shoulder and criticizing every

PUNISHMENT

move she made. And to make the day even better, the men would be planting in the fields on the other side of the woods. That meant that Sara would have to pack their dinner for them to take as they wouldn't be home for the noon meal. Sara went to bed that night with something to be thankful for and a smile on her face. She looked forward to the next day.

CHAPTER FOUR

CAUGHT

The next day was sunny and hot. Sara worked hard to get through her chores as quickly as possible. Mrs. Haley had left for the day with the warning that she would be back at suppertime and all should be ready. Sara planned a meal that would not take long to prepare. If she worked quickly enough, she could have a few hours to call her own and enjoy some time off. She worked through the morning on the washing and filled the clothesline. Washing clothes was a hot and tiresome job. Afterwards, she scrubbed the kitchen floor. She worked straight through lunch since she had packed dinner pails for the men, and they wouldn't be back until suppertime. As she scrubbed the floor, she felt the heat and became slightly lightheaded. She had not taken time for breakfast or lunch. As soon as she was done scrubbing the floor, she would head for the creek and the cool water. Then she would return and eat and enjoy the afternoon.

CAUGHT

The creek felt so refreshing. Sara reveled in the coolness of the water on her feet as she dipped them in the creek. She loosened her braids and freed her long hair from its confinement. She wanted to simply lean back on a tree and doze, but she knew if she did, she would never wake up in time as she felt so tired. She watched the water flow briskly downstream. She dropped a leaf in the water and watched it swirl as the water carried it along. It was caught in a whirlpool and went round and round, then it dropped out of sight under the water.

Sara slowly stood up and started to braid her hair loosely. She would head back to the house and do it properly with a brush. She still would have a couple of hours to do some crocheting before she had to start supper.

Sara left the creek and the coolness of the woods behind her and started back to the house. Her stomach ached from the lack of food, but she felt better than she had before. She was walking past the barn when she heard a step behind her. She turned only to find Jud bearing down on her.

"Jud. What are you doing here? I thought you were working in the far field today." Sara slowly began backing up.

Jud stepped closer. "I had to come back to make a repair. But what do I find, but a pretty thing sunning by the creek."

"I have to go back to the house. I still have chores waiting for me." Sara turned to go, but Jud grabbed her and pulled her to him.

"Not so fast, Sara. I think it is time for you and me to really get to know each other." Jud started pulling her through the barn door.

"No, Jud. Let me go!" Sara squirmed and fought, but Jud was so much stronger that he half carried her inside. Sara started to scream, but Jud simply laughed at her.

"There's no one to hear you, Sara, just me."

Jud threw her on the straw in the corner of one of the stalls. She hit her head against the side of the stall when she landed. Sara prayed for help, but Jud loomed over her. Her head was throbbing. All she could see was the burning desire in his eyes. Everything around her started to whirl. She suddenly felt like the leaf in the creek, she was being carried along by the flowing water. Now she was in a whirlpool with everything spinning around her. Her last thought was, *Lord, give me strength to fight,* but Jud had pinned her down. He leaned closer to kiss her. That's when everything went black.

When Sara came to again, she found herself alone. Her blouse was torn and her body felt bruised and abused. Jud was nowhere to be seen. Sara sat up against the protest of her body. She hurt deep within. Suddenly nauseated, she turned to the side as her body rejected the acid in her stomach. Not having had any food, she convulsed with dry heaves that left her drained and weak.

Why, Lord? Sara questioned. *Where was Your protection? Was this part of your plan for my life? Wasn't it hard enough before this? Have you simply forsaken me?* Sara tasted salt on her lips and realized she was crying. How could she go on? Her life would never be the same. She wished it would just end now. But go on she must. Go on as if this had never happened. How was she going to face Jud? *Lord, I can't do this. I do not have the strength or the courage. Father always said You could make beauty from ashes, that You could use anything that happened to us, good or bad, and use it for our good and Your glory.* Sara wiped the tears from her face and grimaced. *I think You have Your work cut out for You this time.*

Sara rose to her feet. She started to the house. Her body screamed from the pain within her and her stomach felt like it was in knots. When she reached the house, she began pumping water into the bucket and carried it into the storeroom and dumped the water into a washtub. After two more trips to refill the bucket, Sara closed the door and rolled the barrel in front of it. She undressed and slowly began bathing herself. Bruises were starting to appear on her arms and legs. Carefully and gently, she washed herself, hurting many places in the process. After she finished, she dressed, putting on a long sleeved blouse to cover the bruising on her arms. It would be hot, but she figured Mrs. Haley wouldn't really notice that much and she didn't want to have to explain the bruises to anyone.

She didn't feel any cleaner after the bathing, but that's the way it was. She couldn't change what had happened; she could only go on one step at a time. She moved the barrel and opened the door. She emptied the tub and hung it up to dry. Then she went back out to the clothesline to see if the clothes were dry. Carrying in the ones that were, she folded them, separating the ones that needed to be ironed. Setting the hot-irons on the stove she got out the ironing board and worked at the ironing.

She prepared a stew for supper and would fix some biscuits to go with it. She worked mechanically without thinking. She heard Mrs. Haley return with the buggy and heard her shout for her. Sara knew she wanted her to carry in the supplies she had bought. Sara also knew she would be in for a scolding, but somehow she couldn't make her feet move from the spot where she stood in the kitchen. She didn't care. She had a throbbing headache. She knew she had to eat something so she ate half a slice of bread. Although she found it hard to swallow, she gulped it down and drank some water.

Mrs. Haley stomped into the kitchen. "Sara, didn't you hear me call? I have several packages out in the buggy which need to be carried into the house. . ." her voice trailed off.

"Sara, what is wrong with you? Are you ill? What have you been doing?"

Sara stared at the woman as though she hadn't spoken. Her limbs started to shake and Sara felt that she was going to melt to the floor. For the first time in all the years Sara had lived in this house, Mrs. Haley reached out for her and put her arms around her and helped her into the storeroom and her bed.

CHAPTER FIVE
COMPLICATION

Sara's days ran together for the next few weeks. She had hardly said two words to anybody the entire month of June. Surprisingly enough, Mrs. Haley had not given her a bad time about anything. Jud simply ignored her as though she was beneath him. He had taken up to going into town where he was courting one of the town girls.

Sara felt rather numb and went through each day mechanically. Even at night, she said her prayers as though they were written and memorized. She had little or no feeling as she said them, but she knew they were the best she could do for right now. A month had gone by without any further incident, except that Sara started to feel queasy from time to time.

In July, she didn't feel well. The first morning that the smell of the bacon frying caused her stomach to churn, she barely made it outside behind the large lilac bush before she was sick. The next day it was the smell of sausage browning and she repeated her trip to the lilac bush. The third day, she hadn't even started to cook when she quickly dashed outside. At first, she thought she might have eaten something that hadn't set well with her, but by the third day she wasn't sure. By lunchtime the sickening feeling in the pit of her stomach had lessened and by late afternoon she felt fine. It was just the mornings she had trouble getting through.

It was well into the third week of being ill in the mornings, that Mrs. Haley caught her being sick. Then it became very plain to Sara what was wrong.

"Are you feverish?" asked Mrs. Haley. "Have you been throwing up in the mornings?"

When Sara admitted that she had been, Mrs. Haley really became aggravated.

"Have you been fooling around on the sly?" Mrs. Haley asked the question, but she knew Sara had not been anywhere. The only time she was out of sight was at night when they went to bed. But Mrs. Haley didn't want to face the answer that was obvious.

Sara simply looked at her in silence. She knew Mrs. Haley would never believe the truth, or she would ignore it if she thought it might be true.

"I can't have someone working for me who lacks morals and is going to have an illegitimate child. It is just as well that you will be leaving soon. But understand me, girl, I don't want one word of this to get out to anyone, not even the men-folk, or I will make your life a living nightmare!" With that she turned and left Sara standing in the kitchen.

It was at that moment Sara realized that she was indeed with child. *Lord, I don't understand why You are allowing this to happen to me. Now what do I do?*

Suddenly Sara thought of Jud. What would he do when he found out? She couldn't let him ever find out. Sara knew then that she had to get away, far away, and soon, very soon. *Lord, help me to plan, to know what I should do. Give me direction and lead me. Lord, I'm so frightened. Frightened to stay, frightened to go, frightened of what the day holds and frightened at the thought of tomorrow. Frightened to take the next step, whatever it is. Lord, I need your strength and your leading.*

Slowly, Sara turned back to the stove and finished fixing the breakfast meal. She placed everything on the table and promptly left the kitchen. She went to the garden and started working in the vegetable patch. She would no longer eat meals with the Haleys. She would simply avoid them as much as she could. Right now she needed to think and plan. August would soon be upon them and they would be busy with canning while the men were busy getting ready for the harvest. She needed enough time to think and plan. But she didn't want to stay any longer than she had to as she wanted to leave this farm far behind.

COMPLICATION

Fall came on early. The harvesting was almost finished. All the fruits and vegetables had been canned and the storeroom held a bounty for the Haley family. Sara was still at the Haley farm. She and Mrs. Haley barely spoke to each other. Sara showed no evidence of her pregnancy, but she was aware there was a new life within her. She felt a flutter now and then in the depths of her stomach. She now realized that her flight had to take into consideration the life within her. It was the main reason she had not left yet. Oddly enough, Mrs. Haley had not pushed her to leave.

Sara had been taking as many collars to the store as she could possibly make. She had a small nest egg squirreled away. She had taken inventory of her possessions and added to her meager store. She had a dress, a skirt, two blouses, a nightgown and one apron. She had a winter cloak and a shawl. She only had one cloth bonnet, but a hat just wasn't practical. She still had her portmanteau she had brought from her father's house and her father's Bible. It wasn't much, but she couldn't have handled much more.

"Sara!" Mrs. Haley's voice certainly had a way of carrying. Sara was in the storeroom, so she hurried out to the kitchen to see what Mrs. Haley wanted.

"Sara, I think the time has come for you to make plans to leave. I think you should go to another town far away so your *condition* isn't known by others here. I realize that you may need some assistance. I have arranged by letter for you to room with an acquaintance of mine. She will help you through this time and the delivery. After the child is born, she'll make arrangements for adoption and you'll be free to go."

"Free to go? Give up the baby for adoption?"

"Come now, it's the best plan there is. You could never make it on your own in your condition or with a newborn baby. I've made these arrangements with your best interests in mind. I will even handle the costs."

"Why would you want to pay for my room and board until the baby comes? That is not like you."

"Not like me? Why I feel that as a Christian woman, it is the only charitable thing I could do. I only ask that you promise you will never come back to this town or area again."

Sara simply stared at her. She knew Mrs. Haley was not a Christian in the true sense of the word, and she was not charitable in any sense of that word. She only did what would profit her.

Since Sara didn't speak, Mrs. Haley finished with, "Then I take it that we are in agreement. You will be leaving in two weeks' time. The lady lives about 150 miles east of here. She will expect some light housework and chores from you. Until then, remember, you promised not to say a word to anyone." With that, Mrs. Haley turned and went into the hallway and upstairs to her room.

COMPLICATION

Sara pulled out a kitchen chair and sat down. What was Mrs. Haley up to now? Then Sara realized that Mrs. Haley knew Sara had not been seeing anyone. She knew who had taken advantage of Sara. Jud! Suddenly Sara sat up as she also realized that Mrs. Haley knew this baby would be her grandchild. Sara was sure she knew who would be *adopting* the baby. Mrs. Haley wanted the baby, but not Sara!

This changes everything, thought Sara. I've got to act and act now. I need to go now, this very night. *Lord, guide my thoughts and my plans. Make me wise and not foolish in what I do. Thank you, for helping me to understand what's going on.* Sara put her chin in her hand and started thinking. Several ideas came to her. A plan started to form. She knew she had to plan wisely; she did not want Mrs. Haley or Jud to find her. She knew inside her very being, they would take the baby away from her.

CHAPTER SIX

FLIGHT

*S*ara tried to rest while she waited for the household to go to sleep. She waited for the silence that told her all had gone to bed. Then she continued to wait. While she did so, she prayed. *Oh, Lord, I have many doubts and fears over what I'm about to do, but I am trusting in You to take those away and give me Your peace. Direct my steps, guide my feet in Thy paths and keep me from going astray. Protect me, Lord, from evil and harm that may wait for me. Touch me with Thy wisdom, and lead my decisions according to Thy will. I pray for this household, this family, Lord. I know they don't know you, Jesus, and I pray they will know You personally someday. Lord, help me to forgive them for the harm they have done. I look to you, Lord, to bless this life within me. I know I would not have chosen the circumstances, but You knew this life within me, before I did. You have already planned his or her life, and I pray that whatever may come to this one I carry, that he or she will know You as Savior. Now Father,*

FLIGHT

I thank You for Your Son, who saved me, and it is in His name I pray. Amen.

Sara opened her eyes and felt at peace within herself and rested. Quietly she got up and checked to make sure she had packed everything she was taking. Outside of her clothes and Bible, there was nothing else, except a couple of biscuits she had pocketed at suppertime. She thought about taking some of the canned goods, but decided against it. Her heavenly Father would provide, and she needed to trust Him.

Slowly she rolled the barrel away from the door without making any noise. She went through the doorway and closed the door behind her. She carefully walked through the kitchen and out the back door. She made a quick stop at the small building out back and then walked on down the road. She listened for a yell or any sign that someone saw or heard her leaving, but the night remained quiet with only the sounds of the night creatures rustling in the grasses. She had first considered walking into town and catching the stage from there. Yet the more she considered it, the more she realized it would be the first place they would look for her. She decided not to go the direction of town, but go overland and meet the stage several miles from town on the road heading north. She hoped she could wave them to a stop and pay her passage at the next town.

Sara knew she had several miles to walk before she got to the main road leading north. She hoped they would think she headed east or west on the train or the second stage that came through town. Sara stepped out at a steady pace, but didn't push herself as she knew it would be a long night and she would tire eventually. Her portmanteau was a good weight, but not as heavy as it would have been if she had canned food. She would wait until it was almost morning, before she would eat her biscuits. She was so thankful she was no longer fighting morning sickness.

Sara walked all night. She had no idea how many miles she covered or exactly where she would come out onto the road. She heard barking dogs, but they were at a distance. An occasional owl hooted from a tree and she heard others as well from time to time. Just before sunrise, she came to a small stream. The water looked refreshing and Sara splashed it upon her face. Then she sat and ate her biscuits, washing them down with the cool water. After resting for a few more moments, she picked up her portmanteau and waded across the stream and continued on her way. She came to a clump of oak trees when she saw the road ahead. *Thank you, Lord. Now help me to flag down the stagecoach and let there be room enough for me to ride.*

Sara wasn't sure how long the stage would take to reach this point, but she knew it was to leave town at early morning if it wasn't running late. She was certain it would not have been here yet even if it was running on schedule. She found a place among the trees where she could sit and rest and yet see the road well enough that when she spotted the stage, she would be able to grab her things and get to the road long before the stage would come upon her.

As Sara rested, she found herself jerking awake when she had dozed off. This will never do, she thought. She sat up a little straighter so that she wasn't quite as comfortable. The dawn was breaking beautifully. Sara opened her portmanteau and took out her Bible. She would read and pray. There was no better way to start the day. She read for a while and again prayed for her Father's guidance. She had no sooner slipped her Bible back into the valise when she heard horses. Looking up she saw the stage coming and she quickly picked up her things and hurried to the road. She waved and saw the horses were slowing and then stopping.

"Can I be of assistance, Ma'am?" asked the driver.

"May I get a seat on the stage? I can pay for the ticket at the next town or now, if you like," she asked as she looked up at him.

"I think it will be all right to do that when we reach our next stop. We're running the mail today. Hop up into the coach. If'n you need help, I'll be glad to do so."

"Thank you. I think I can manage." Sara got the door open and was able to get inside the coach without help. As soon as she shut the door the driver called to the team and the coach started forward with a jerk. Sara settled back in a seat. She was alone. Once again she closed her eyes and thanked her heavenly Father for the solitude. Then she promptly dozed off as the coach rocked back and forth. An occasional bump or jerk occurred, but it didn't disturb her. Sara slept on undisturbed even when the driver started singing at the top of his lungs. It was just as well.

CHAPTER SEVEN

DREAM

The train moved along with a steady clickety-clack. It had been a long trip. Sara had ridden the coach for two days in a northerly direction, and then caught another stage line to the next town west, where she could connect with a train going west. So far, there had been no sign of pursuit.

Sara felt like every bone in her body had been abused from the jarring of the stage. The first night's stopover, she had found a room at a boarding house and got some rest. The second night, she shared a room with another female rider as most rooms were taken. That was a lot easier on her money as it was dwindling. However, the other lady, much older, was a snorer and Sara's night was not as restful, leaving her tired. She didn't have money for meals, so she was ordering milk when she could, and bought cheese and crackers to nibble on when her stomach growled from the emptiness. Until she had purchased a train ticket west, she was afraid to use any more money than she absolutely had to spend.

Finally she had reached the connection for the train and bought a ticket as far west as she could afford. It didn't leave her any money at all except for a few pennies, but she could stay on the train at night and didn't have to get lodgings. Sara relaxed. At least for the time being, she was safe from Jud.

O Lord, let me trust You and not let my fear of Jud have control in my life. Sara knew that though Jud had ignored her after he had attacked her in the barn, he would not let her go, especially if his mother told him she was pregnant. For now, she needn't worry about him sneaking up on her. *Lord, once again, I give my fears to You. Clear the memory of the attack from my thoughts. Help me to dwell on You and not on my own suffering. It becomes nothing when I consider all that You suffered on the cross for me.* Sara tipped her head against the side of the car. The lack of sleep combined with the steady rhythm of the train lulled her to sleep. Soon she was dreaming.

Sara dreamed she arrived at a small town and there found a home and friends. She found a job as a seamstress. She felt safe and secure and happy for the first time since she had lost her father. She heard the Lord speak to her, *Rest, my child, rest.*

All was going well until there was a commotion in town. Suddenly, Jud appeared and rode into town on a large black stallion shouting

Sara's name. Sara panicked. All rest was gone, her friends disappeared, and Sara found herself standing in the middle of the street alone facing the approaching Jud.

Trust me. I will keep you safe and deliver you. Sara heard the Lord speak to her once more. Jud kept riding towards her and she could see the anger in his face and the determination in the set of his jaw. He was going to have her, to own her. The closer he got, the harder her heart beat and her breath came faster and faster.

Trust me, sounded in her head. *Alright, Lord, I'll stand still and trust in You to care for me.* Jud was getting so close now that Sara could see his eyes glaring at her. She stood her ground telling herself to trust in the Lord to deliver her. She couldn't move and simply waited. Jud rode up to her and passed her by as though she was invisible. She quickly turned to watch him, but he was gone! He had disappeared as quickly as he had appeared.

Sara started, awoke and sat up. The dream had been so real. Her heart was still pounding. As she sat there, Sara felt a gentle peace settle over her. The train steadily rolled along assuring her that she was still heading west. She knew the Lord was indeed telling her to rest and trust in Him. She now knew He would care for her no matter what lay ahead.

CHAPTER EIGHT

STOPOVER

Sara continued going west on the train for two more days. She knew she needed to find a place to stay and some work in order to replenish her exhausted funds. The trip had been tiring and her back ached. She had eaten very little and was a little queasy at her stomach. She needed a good meal and soon.

"Next stop – Fulbright!" announced the conductor as he moved through the car.

"Excuse me, sir," Sara said as the conductor came abreast of her seat.

"Yes, Miss, may I help you?" he said as he paused.

"Will there be a lay-over in Fulbright?"

"Yes, Miss. We'll be stopping for the lunch hour."

"Thank you, sir," said Sara. She sat back in her seat while the conductor moved on through the car and into the next one. Sara was thinking and praying. She felt the Lord was trying to tell her something through her dream. Sara checked to make sure everything she had was gathered and put into her portmanteau. It and her small handbag was all of the luggage she had to carry. She would get off at Fulbright and look around. If she decided to stay, her luggage would be with her.

The engine's whistle blew and the train started slowing down until it finally halted at the station. Sara took a deep breath, picked up her grip and slowly moved to the doorway of the passenger coach. She stepped down off the train onto the depot platform. Quietly, she walked through the bustling depot to the opposite doorway which led outside onto the busy main street of a small town. From where she stood, it looked like the depot was at one end of the town, so Sara turned and started walking down the street.

She passed the first storefront that simply said, "EATS." She looked inside, then quickly walked on past it. Not even starvation could drive her to eat in a place that dirty and greasy looking.

Sara continued down the street passing a feed and hardware store as well as a livery. Across the street was a large store where she read "Huston's Emporium" over its porch area. As she headed that direction, she stepped carefully around the markers that were common in the dirt streets of horse drawn vehicles. When she stepped up on the clapboard walk, she noticed a "HELP WANTED" sign in the left hand window next to the front double doors.

In smaller letters was written, "Inquire within." Sara opened the door.

The first thing Sara recognized was the aromas of a grocery. Freshly ground coffee beans, the dill vinegary brine from the pickle barrel, cinnamon, cloves and other spices filled the air. Mixed with these were the smells of leather goods and soaps.

The emporium was a large store, housing everything one would need on a homestead of any size. Food, clothing, boots and shoes, jewelry, books, bolts of cloth, men and women's hats, as well as tools, buckets, washtubs, stoves, furniture, etc. Every space, high or low, was used. She thought it was a wonder that anyone could know where anything was located.

Sara stepped aside as a customer approached the door to leave. She watched the clerks, a man and a woman, who seemed to have no problem locating the items that their customers requested. After ten minutes or so, business slowed down and she approached the woman.

"May I help you?" queried the lady.

"Yes. I noticed your "HELP WANTED" sign in the window," Sara hesitated, then finished with, "and I wondered what kind of help was needed."

"Oh, that. My husband, Henry, is looking for a stock boy or man to help with the heavy lifting and carrying."

"I see. Thank you," responded a disappointed Sara.

"Is there anything I can get for you?" asked the clerk.

"Could I please have a small slice of your cheese and a small sack of crackers?" asked Sara.

"Certainly." The woman quickly sliced the cheese and wrapped it in brown paper. Then she put a handful of crackers in a small poke and brought them to Sara. "That will be six cents, please."

Sara dug in her coin pouch and came up with enough pennies to pay for the meager rations.

"Thank you," said the clerk as she put the coins in the till. She hesitated, then turned and put out her hand to Sara. "I'm Betty, by the by. That's my husband, Henry. Welcome to Fulbright."

Sara returned the handshake and smile. "I'm Sara."

"Sara, are you looking for work?" asked Betty.

"Yes, I am. I've not done much. I know how to cook, keep a house, and crochet fancy collars for ladies," offered Sara.

"Come with me," said Betty. She caught Henry's attention and pointed to the ceiling. He nodded and Betty led the way to a door at the back of the store on the left. The door led to a long narrow storage room with a back door and a stairway off to the left that led upstairs.

Betty started up the stairs that were lit by a small window. At the top was a short hallway with another small window, and two doors on the left. The first door said *Office* and was bypassed. Betty stopped at the second door towards the end, unlocked it and entered with Sara following close behind.

Inside was an apartment that covered the top floor. It had very roomy proportions. The first room was the parlor or sitting room with three windows to the right overlooking the street in front of the store. It had a door on the opposite wall, which Betty said led to their spare bedroom. At the end of the room was a large archway that led into the dining room. It had two windows facing the street and was not as large as the parlor. It also had a door opposite the windows which led to the master bedroom. The door across from the archway was a swinging door and led into a small kitchen. The kitchen had a window facing the street and the opposite door opened to reveal a small walk-in pantry. The kitchen had all the modern conveniences with lots of cupboard space.

Betty also took Sara to the two bedrooms to view and she saw each of them had closets as well as windows that faced the back of the building.

"The apartment is wonderful," remarked Sara.

"It's home and it's definitely convenient for work. Henry tried to make it as modern as he could and we don't feel cramped for space. Now, if we end up with several children, we both may want an actual house, but for now, this is perfect for us. Come back into the kitchen and let me fix us both a cup of tea. I have a proposition to offer you."

Betty led the way back into the kitchen. The train whistle could be heard down the street announcing its soon departure. Sara wondered if she should go or stay to see what Betty wanted to ask. *Lead me, Lord.* It was then she realized she had a peace about staying in this town. The train whistle sounded again. Sara smiled to herself. She was staying.

CHAPTER NINE

PROPOSITION

Betty set the tea things on the dining room table and poured for both of them. "Now, Sara, I won't keep you wondering why I brought you up here. As you can see, the apartment is large and fine, but it needs a good cleaning to say the least. You see, I was the third oldest of four daughters to a storekeeper back in Ohio. I loved being a clerk in a store since the very first. My sisters didn't. So I went to the store each day with Father and the others stayed home with Mother. Consequently, they know how to cook and keep house, I know how to run a store.

"Henry and I met at the store. When he proposed to me, I warned him that I wanted to clerk, not house-keep, and he said that was fine with him. But it isn't fine, especially when we both end a tiring day and come up here to find nothing hot and ready to eat. Poor Henry doesn't complain, though. I only wish we had a good place to eat in town, but *EATS* isn't the place.

"My proposition is this; would you be interested in coming to work for us up here in the apartment? You could clean and do the housekeeping, bake and cook hot meals for us, and crochet collars in your spare time."

Sara immediately thought *Thank you, Lord! Thank you!* "Yes, I would be very happy to cook and clean for you. This is an answer to prayer for me."

"Wonderful!" exclaimed Betty with a clap of her hands. "Now we need to get you settled somewhere to stay. I would offer our spare bedroom, but Henry's brother is due to join us any time now and he will stay with us. That will be three people for you to look after, is that alright?"

"I don't see a problem with that. But in all fairness, I don't know how long I will be able to stay. It could be a few weeks or forever. I don't know just yet."

"I'll take you as long as you can stay. If there is anything I can do to make you want to stay, I'll do it. I think the next thing we need to do is to get you settled at Flo's. She is a young widow who runs a boarding house to make her living. She's very nice and a great friend. I'll send you to Flo's boarding house to get a room, settle in, rest and eat a good meal. Flo is a good cook and doesn't tolerate any nonsense. Our town's sheriff is sweet on her, so he checks in on her quite often and sees that no one gives her trouble."

"It sounds too good to be true," admitted Sara.

"Then I'll send you over there now and I'll get back downstairs to Henry. If you need a day or two to rest, I'll understand."

"Oh, no, that won't be necessary. I can start tomorrow if you like," insisted Sara.

"I like! Tomorrow will be fine. Say about nine o'clock. You can work until mid-afternoon and stop, if you can leave dinner in the oven or on the stove for us. We can work that out as we go along, I think." Betty led the way back out of the apartment and locked the door. "I'll have a key ready for you tomorrow. Since our back door is often open for deliveries, Henry prefers to keep the apartment locked. Our store office is this other door, but Henry usually works in there of an evening or a very slow day. You tell Flo that I sent you and you are going to work for me. Tell her I said the first week's board will be paid by the store. After that, you can pay for it out of your wages."

"Thank you. You are so kind. I wasn't sure how I was going to pay for my room," admitted Sara. *Lord, You have provided again. Thank you.*

Sara walked further down the street until the stores ended and the houses began. The second house on the other side of the street was Flo's. It was a two-story clapboard with a deep porch on the front. The yard was small with a tree in the side yard that offered shade.

Sara liked the look of the place and liked the owner even more when she answered her knock. Flo stood every bit of four feet eleven inches tall and was a tiny fireball in both her attitude and her red hair. After Sara mentioned that Betty had sent her, Flo said she was delighted to have her as a boarder. She led Sara upstairs and let her select a front room or one in the back. Sara took the front room.

"The necessary is out back. Supper's at six. If'n you'd like to lie down and rest, I'll call you about fifteen minutes beforehand."

"Thank you. That sounds like a great idea."

"Good. I will see you later then. If there is anything you need, let me know." With that, Flo took herself off and returned to her kitchen downstairs.

Sara unpacked her few things and nibbled on her crackers and cheese. There was a slight breeze coming through the windows. She was so tired that she fell asleep almost as soon as she rested her head on the pillow.

CHAPTER TEN

BOARDERS

Sara was startled awake by the tapping on her door.

"Dinner in fifteen minutes, Sara." Flo's retreating footsteps could be heard as she went back downstairs.

Sara blinked and looked around the room as though she was seeing it for the first time. The room had two windows, one facing the street and the other the side yard. A double bed, a chest of drawers, a small table with a bowl and pitcher and towel next to it, a bedside table and a chair made up the furniture in the room. There were hooks on the back of the door to hang clothes. The walls were papered in a small flowered print and the only light in the room was the oil lamp that set on the bedside table. Already the light had faded as the days were getting shorter.

Sara went to the mirror that hung above the table with the bowl and pitcher. She looked into it to see a pale drawn face that was mostly brown eyes staring back at her. She poured some water from the pitcher into the bowl and washed the sleep from her eyes. She patted her hair back into place and straightened her skirt. She was as ready as she ever was going to be and she quietly slipped out of her room and down the stairs.

The smells of dinner greeted her first. Once again she felt the pangs of hunger, but at least, this time, she was going to do something about it. As she entered the parlor, two gentlemen stood. About that time, Flo entered the room and introduced them.

The short stocky man with the balding head and glasses was a Mr. Phillip Tyson, a salesman. Mr. Tyson was in town for a few days as he was traveling west from town to town selling *Mr. Jacoby's Homeopathic Remedies*. The second man, Mr. Horace Canton, was of medium height, but very thin, and was the local school master. Flo told them that Miss Morrow had recently arrived and would be part of their household for the time being.

Flo then led the way into the dining room and everyone was seated. The food was simple, but nourishing, and Sara enjoyed every bite. There wasn't much chatter as they ate, which suited Sara, who was more interested in the food than the conversation. After the meal, the gentlemen returned to the parlor, but Sara stayed behind and offered to help Flo with the dishes.

"I appreciate the offer, but I can handle everything from here. Breakfast is served about 7:30 in the morning. I ring a bell ten minutes before it's served. Lunch is on your own, unless you order a lunch, which Mr. Canton does. I charge extra for that."

"That won't be necessary," insisted Sara. "Thank you again for dinner. It was very good."

"You're welcome. If there is anything you need, let me know." Flo picked up the plates she had gathered and went through the doorway to the kitchen.

Sara decided she didn't want to join the gentlemen in the parlor, so she headed back upstairs to her room. She decided to go to bed early. Surprisingly, she fell asleep almost immediately and slept through until morning.

When she first woke up, she couldn't figure out where she was. But soon she heard a wagon going by and remembered the events of yesterday. Today would be her first day working for the Hustons. She dressed quickly and braided her hair wrapping the braids around her head and pinning them in place. She had just finished when she heard the bell for breakfast. Sara quickly made her bed and tidied the room, then headed downstairs.

After nodding and bidding the two gentlemen good morning, Sara enjoyed the eggs and biscuits Flo had made. After breakfast, she went back upstairs and spent some time reading her Bible and asking the Lord to bless her day. *Lord, help me to lean on You and trust You to watch over me. Give me the strength for the tasks today, and I thank You for this room and the work that I have to do. Amen.*

Sara stood up. It was time. A new adventure was before her. A slight flutter in her stomach reminded her of her situation. *Lord, please bless this little one. Keep it healthy and direct our path. Amen.* Sara was ready and left for the Emporium.

CHAPTER ELEVEN

DISCOVERY

Sara had been working for the Hustons for several weeks. She had gotten to know Betty and Flo quite well as the three of them would sometimes have afternoon tea together. So far, Henry's brother hadn't shown, but was still expected. Sundays, the Hustons usually came to Flo's for the noon meal and visit. The men would go to the parlor to discuss various political topics, but the three ladies would congregate in the kitchen helping Flo clean up and wash dishes. Chattering the whole time, they enjoyed each other's company and a friendship blossomed between them. The circuit preacher only came every third Sunday, so Sara had not yet attended church.

It was on a Tuesday morning, that Sara arrived at the Huston's apartment only to find Betty violently ill. She said she hadn't been able to keep anything down lately in the mornings. Sara smiled at her and made her some tea and went downstairs long enough to get some crackers and bring them up to Betty.

"Try drinking this and nibble on a few crackers now and then. I dare say that you will be feeling better by the afternoon." Sara smiled at her.

"Do you know what is wrong with me?" asked a very pale Betty.

"When did you last have your monthlies?" Sara returned.

"Not since, since two or more months ago. Sara, do you mean – do you think I'm in the family way?"

"I wouldn't be surprised. But then, I'm not a doctor. I just know what you're going through."

"What do you mean, you know? Have you gone through this before?"

Sara hung her head and stood up, turning away from her friend. She hadn't meant to tell anyone, but Betty had been so good to her. *Lord, I need Your leading here. I want to talk to someone about what I'm going through. Lord, You brought me here, maybe just for this moment. Please guide my words.*

Sara faced Betty again and quietly told her story. She explained how she had been sick and Mrs. Haley had caught her and told her what it meant. She explained how she was being pushed to give up the baby, so Mrs. Haley could adopt it. She told her how she feared Jud, and was certain he was or would be looking for her.

"I came here by the Lord's leading. I was exhausted, hungry and out of money. I was desperate to find rest and safety. And thanks to you and Henry, I have it, at least for a little while."

Betty ventured, "Do you think Jud will trace you here?"

Sara nodded. "He's certain to do it. I don't think I've traveled far enough to evade his discovery. Especially once they are done with harvest and he has time. He'll be looking, I am certain of it."

"Well, I hope you're right about a baby for Henry and me, and wrong about Jud finding you. But what will you do if he shows up in Fulbright?"

"I don't know. I need to be making some plans. But I don't want to go out and about too much or someone will identify me. If I purchase a ticket, I'm afraid the ticket agent will recognize my description and tell Jud where I'm headed. Somehow, I need to plan a way to get out of town without Jud knowing I was ever here."

"That's a tough puzzle, but maybe we can come up with a plan. If you're willing for Flo to know, we could put our three heads together. Surely the three of us can come up with a plan."

"That would be great, but I sure hate the thought of leaving Fulbright and my two friends behind. Where can I go? What can I do? Sometimes it seems so overwhelming, that all I can do is put it in the Lord's hands."

"That's the best place to leave it. But Flo and I can help you and the Lord out a little. I am getting an idea . . . that I'm going to be sick

DISCOVERY

again!" With that Betty flew back into the bedroom. When she came out, looking paler than ever, Sara encouraged her to lie down and put a cold cloth on her head.

Betty admitted that the smell of bacon frying was what had started her being sick today.

"Smells will do that. I found any kind of grease or fried foods would set me off. The crackers settle on one's stomach the best. But I'm afraid it will last a few weeks before it passes."

"You mean it won't last the whole time I'm pregnant?" asked a hopeful Betty.

"Not that I know. I was sick about three weeks, and then it started getting better. I'm seldom sick like that now."

"Oh, Sara, I'm so excited about having a baby. Henry and I have wanted one for years, but nothing. Now – I can hardly believe it. I'll have to see the doctor in the next town. We don't have one here yet. We're hoping to have one come before winter. I sure would feel better knowing there was one right here in Fulbright. Mrs. McCurdy is the local mid-wife, and she's a nice lady, but I would like to have a doctor."

"I understand what you mean. It is a scary prospect, but an exciting thing to think about – having a baby. I'm afraid I haven't thought too much about it, I've been so busy trying to hide so Jud won't find me. I guess I had better start making some plans about the baby as well."

"Well, the first step is to come up with an escape plan in case he shows up here. Why don't you ask Flo to come to tea tomorrow afternoon about one o'clock. Hopefully, I'll be feeling better. Let's see what we can come up with if we put our heads together. I'm sure there's a way to do it."

"Betty," replied Sara, "why don't you not worry about me so much and go in and lie down. You look pale, and it might help the sickness to pass. I will let Henry know you will not be clerking today, at least not this morning for sure. I'll work in the kitchen today and will try not to disturb you."

"I think that sounds great. I'll tell Henry about the baby when I've been to a doctor and know for sure. I don't want to get his hopes up for nothing. I'll need to pick up a train ticket to the next town." Betty suddenly turned a little green and added, "Maybe I'll feel like doing that later this afternoon. I'm going back to the bedroom." She disappeared into the bedroom. After a few minutes, Sara went in to clean up and emptied the bowl for Betty. She had already dozed off. Sara smiled and quietly left the room, gently closing the door.

CHAPTER TWELVE

CONSPIRATORS

It wasn't until the following Sunday that the three ladies were able to put their heads together. Sara had told Flo about her situation, but she had not told her about Betty's latest development. Actually, Betty had gone to Culver the next day and came home to tell Henry that yes, indeed, she was expecting. Flo was delighted at the news and for the first part of the hour, they chattered about babies, what was needed, etc. Then Flo changed the subject to Sara and an escape plan for her.

"I have already come up with a great idea," exclaimed Flo. "In order for Sara to move about and board the train, I thought she could have my mourning dress with the hat and veil that I wore when I lost my Hampton. No one would readily recognize her then."

"That's a great idea," said Betty. "I thought maybe you or I could buy the ticket for Sara. That way she couldn't be identified with the ticket and where she is going."

"But where should I go?" asked Sara.

Flo's face lightened, "We'll buy you a ticket as far as you can go. But you should get off at one of the towns you come to before the end of the line. Then take a stagecoach to another town. That should confuse anyone trying to find you."

The three friends talked the plan over trying to find any flaws. They discussed how to proceed if Sara was working upstairs at the Emporium, or she was in her room at Flo's. Sara described Jud to them in detail, as well as his mother, in case she was with him or came on her own. Betty had thought to pick up a train schedule on her trip to Culver and they studied it thoroughly. Plans were made and Sara admitted that she felt a lot more secure knowing that they were there to help. They promised to keep in touch whenever Sara reached where she was going and felt safe enough to correspond with them. Once they had covered everything in their plan, they switched back to the topic of babies and upcoming events.

Later that evening, Flo brought Sara the dress with the black hat and veil. The veil was long and heavy enough, making it difficult to make out Sara's features. The dress was a good fit, but a bit short. Flo said it was a good thing it had a generous hem so they could lengthen it to fit Sara. Sara said she would take it to work the next day and work on it at the Huston apartment when she had time.

"If you are at the Emporium, I'll pack your things and take your portmanteau to the depot shortly before your train leaves. You can pick it up there."

"Oh, Flo, I hope no one comes looking for me. I would like to stay right here at Fulbright. I'll never find better friends than you and Betty. You both have been so wonderful." Sara had tears in her eyes.

Flo gave her a hug. "We can always hope for the best, but it's wise to be prepared for the worse. Now maybe you can sleep a little better tonight than you have been."

Sara did indeed have a restful night's sleep. Again, she dreamed the Lord called to her, *Rest my child, rest. Trust Me.*

The following weeks flew by. Betty was not quite so sick, although she remained queasy at her stomach in the mornings. Somehow, the knowledge that a baby was on the way, made even that queasiness less of a nuisance. Both Henry and Betty beamed and Sara couldn't help but grin at their happiness.

Sara continued cleaning the apartment, but she had reached a point that all of the deep cleaning was done and she was simply doing weekly maintenance cleaning. She cooked and baked for the Hustons and wrote out some simple recipes for Betty to use if and when she had to leave.

By late October, everything had settled back into a routine. Sara had finished the dress and it hung in the spare bedroom at the Emporium. Then, about mid-afternoon, Sara looked out the front parlor window and saw Jud standing across the street looking around the town. Sara froze. She knew he would come. *Rest my child, rest. Trust in Me.* The words went round and round in her mind. The Lord had given them a plan. Now it had to be put into action.

Sara quickly went down the stairs and peeked through the door before opening it completely and motioning for Betty to come to the back.

"Betty, he's here. I just saw him across the street. He seems to be on his own." whispered Sara.

"Don't worry. We have a plan. You go back upstairs and leave everything to Henry and me. I'll get in touch with Flo and we'll plan on you boarding the train tonight. You'll be gone before he can realize that you were here. Remember, very few people in town have met you. Now go back upstairs and be patient. Let me and Flo handle things right now." Betty squeezed Sara's hands and went back into the store, closing the door behind her. Sara took a deep breath, realizing that she could do nothing right now but wait, so she turned and went back upstairs to the apartment. She needed to give her fears to the Lord.

CHAPTER THIRTEEN

DECEPTION

Betty quickly found Henry and whispered in his ear. He nodded and she scooted back over to the grocery side of the store. Moments later, the bell rang as a young man entered the store.

"May I help you?" asked Betty as brightly as possible.

"Maybe so," he answered. "I'm looking for a dear friend that may have stopped here in her travels west. She is about five feet, brown hair and eyes, attractive and well-spoken. Have you seen anyone fitting that description?"

"I can't say that I have, except for some local folk who might fit that description, but no strangers. Henry," Betty called out to her husband, "have you seen any strangers that have brown eyes and hair, about five feet tall, around here?"

"Male or female?" asked Henry.

"Female."

"No, can't say that I have. There was that short salesman, but he was more bald than brown hair."

Betty looked back at the stranger and shrugged. "I'm sorry I can't help you find your friend. Will you be staying in Fulbright long? If you are, and I see her, I can tell her you are looking for her."

"That won't be necessary. I'm not sure how long I'll be staying." The man turned and went back through the door and stood on the porch. Betty noticed he glanced back in at the store, scowled, and then slowly started back across the street to the livery.

"Henry, I need to get a message to Flo. I'd go myself, but something tells me we may be watched."

"Joey Carlson is supposed to stop by after school today. That should be in about twenty minutes. Why don't I send him to Flo's with a delivery? You can slip a message into it."

"Henry, you're a genius. I now know why I married you."

"Is it because I am a genius?"

Betty looked up at him with a frown. "No. It is because you are so outright handsome!" She grinned and scurried to find a pencil and paper.

Betty slipped upstairs and told Sara what had happened. Sara said she had watched him enter the livery, but he hadn't come back out yet. Betty told her Henry's idea of sending Joey with a delivery.

"All we can do now is to wait."

Sara sighed, "That's the hardest part, I think. I guess I need to talk with the Lord some more and keep my mind on Him and not on Jud."

"That's the right spirit!" Betty patted her on her knee and left to return to the store with her message.

Joey came and made the delivery. Flo was a little surprised at getting it, but she asked Joey to wait and quickly opened the package and found the note from Betty. She told Joey to wait as she had an item to take back to the Emporium. She soon returned to the door with a hatbox and a tip for Joey. He grinned and headed back to the store.

Flo went upstairs and packed Sara's things in her portmanteau. There wasn't much to pack, a few clothes, a brush and a Bible. Then Flo carried it downstairs and set it inside the closet under the staircase. She found her reticule and put on her hat. She left her house and quickly headed to the depot. There she purchased a train ticket and checked on the departure time of the evening train. She put the ticket back into her reticule and returned to her house. She put the ticket inside the portmanteau, then she hid it in the closet again and went into the kitchen to start dinner.

Betty had taken the hatbox upstairs to Sara. "Change into the mourning dress, and I'll package up your shirtwaist and skirt. All you will need to do is add them to your portmanteau when you pick it up at the station."

"Betty, do you think this will really work?" asked Sara with a furrowed brow.

"The Lord will make it work," said Betty confidently. *At least for her sake, I hope it works* she thought to herself.

It seemed to Sara that the evening would never come. When it was time to serve the dinner she had fixed for the Hustons, she didn't have much appetite, and ate very little. Betty encouraged her to eat. After dinner, Sara helped her with the dishes.

Suddenly, it was time to leave for the depot. Betty and Sara hugged each other goodbye. Sara put on the hat and veil, picked up the package and headed for the station leaving by the back door and going up the alley.

Meanwhile, Flo had asked Mr. Canton if he would accompany her for a walk to the train station and back. Mr. Canton was very agreeable as Mr. Tyson had long since traveled on and there was no one else to help fill the long evenings. Flo got the portmanteau and Mr. Canton offered to carry it for her. They arrived at the depot about fifteen minutes before the train was to leave. There were a few others getting ready to board as Flo set the portmanteau by the bench in the corner. Just as she turned to leave, a woman in widow's weeds came in and passed her.

Very softly, Flo whispered, "Safe travel," and the woman simply nodded her head. Flo and Mr. Canton went out the other door of the depot and leisurely strolled up the street and back to the boarding house.

Sara looked around to see if anyone was watching. When she felt it was clear, she opened the portmanteau, found the ticket and put her package inside. Closing it back up, she joined the line of passengers boarding the train.

Sara did not notice a man walk up at the far end of the platform, looking over the passengers. It was just as well. If she had seen Jud, she might have reacted and given herself away. As it was, he did not recognize anyone who was boarding the train, and the widow lady never stirred his suspicions as to who she really was. Jud grunted and headed back into town. He was certain he would have found Sara in Fulbright. No one claimed to have seen her. No matter, he'd keep on looking. She couldn't escape him. Jud grinned. Sara would be his again sooner or later. Of that, he was certain.

CHAPTER FOURTEEN

LOST

Fulbright was like a dream to Sara. The time went by so quickly, but the memory of the friendship was still strong. Sara looked out the window of the train. Once again the clickety-clack of the rails tended to mesmerize until the passengers either fell asleep or reached the end of their nerves.

The train had taken a northerly direction. Sara noticed the cold and had her cloak handy when the heat in the car was not a comfortable temperature. She had been riding the train forever, although she had boarded only two nights ago. Tonight would be the third one.

According to the plan the three friends had come up with, Sara would be on the train only one more night. She would arrive at Bloomfield early in the morning. From there she hoped to catch a stage. Of course, that meant she would have to buy a ticket, but with her widow weeds, it wasn't as scary.

Sara hadn't eaten hardly anything the last two days. Betty had stowed some cheese and crackers in the package she had wrapped for her. Sara was ready for something a little more substantial. Sara prayed silently, *Lord, I am in need of nourishment. Please show me a way I can eat and still remain unseen in Bloomfield. Bless Betty and the baby she carries, and bless Flo. Thank You, that I got on this train without Jud being on the same train. Amen.*

Sara told herself she shouldn't have been surprised that at the next scheduled stop, the train would be delayed an hour for repairs. The passengers were encouraged to get off and go into town for a meal. The train would blow the whistle twice before departure. Now she could eat and let it hold her over until she reached her destination.

Sara found a table in a corner and enjoyed beef, potatoes, and cooked apples. She was still in her widow garb and wore it as added protection. She was on her way back to the train when she realized the agent for train tickets also sold for the stage lines. She stopped and inquired if Bloomfield had a stage that came into that town. The agent checked his schedules and said no, the closest stage line for Bloomfield was in the next town which was ten miles north of it. She thanked him and returned to the coach and her seat ten minutes before the train departed. Again, she thanked the Lord for the meal and the rest stop. She thought about what lay ahead. The next town was ten miles north of Bloomfield. She could walk that easily in a day. It would also be another way to hide her intended destination from Jud.

Another lady, with two young children and a baby got on and seated themselves across the aisle from Sara. The little girl was about three, the boy about two, and both were fighting between themselves. Sara could tell the young mother was at her wits end as the baby was fussy as well. She asked the two children if they would like to hear a story. Both of them nodded and moved over to sit across from Sara. She began to tell them the story of David keeping the sheep, fighting the lion and bear, and then the giant. By the time she was close to the end of the story, the little girl was on her lap and the boy was sitting next to her. As soon as she finished, she realized the boy was nodding his head and the little girl kept opening her eyes fighting sleep. She softly sang to them and their eyes closed. She looked over to the mother who mouthed, "Thank you." Sara quietly stood and let the little boy sleep on the seat. The little girl she held as she sat down across from the boy. The girl wasn't heavy, but she was on the warm side. Two hours later at the next town, the mother with the three little ones got off.

Sara slept off and on during the night. The coach was relatively quiet, except for the sound of snoring from a few of the passengers. Sara was awake and praying as the day began to dawn and the conductor came through the car announcing, "Bloomfield, Bloomfield. Coming into Bloomfield." This is it, Sara thought, the next step in my travels, and maybe the last one, God willing.

The train chugged into town and screeched to a halt. Passengers began to disembark. Sara waited her turn, but tried to stay in the middle of the busiest group so she might go unnoticed. As she stepped into the depot, she asked a baggage handler which road out of town was the one to Newton. He told her it was the road that went past the church at the edge of town. He also added that about halfway there, when she came to the fork in the road, to keep to her left, as the road split and the right branch headed up into the mountains. Sara thanked him and moved on.

It was early, but still dark, considering it was morning. Sara looked up at the overcast sky and realized some weather was starting to move into the area. She was glad for her cloak as the air in Bloomfield was quite cold. It will just make for a brisker pace for me and a speedier arrival at Newton, hopefully before the weather set in. Sara walked steadily through the town and had no trouble finding the road leading past the church. She kept moving forward with a light heart resulting from the hope that she had gone far enough that Jud would never find her.

After about two miles, it started to snow. The flakes were light and feathery at first, then the wind picked up and the flakes started to sting her face. Sara pulled the veil down over her face which gave her protection from the snow, but she was still walking into the wind. With her head bent, she trudged on. She was surprised that after another mile, the snow was starting to accumulate and made walking more difficult. She walked on telling herself that she was close to being halfway there. She reasoned it would be foolish to turn back to Bloomfield, and the plan would then be compromised. Sara kept on. The walking became more and more difficult. Although she pulled her cloak close around her, her hands and feet felt so cold. She was starting to lose feeling in them. *Lord, I am in trouble here. Guide me, O Lord, and protect me and the baby. Help us to reach a safe haven. Amen.* Sara thought she might be getting close to the fork in the road and she didn't want to miss it. She couldn't see well through the veil, so she started to lift it off her face. A gust of wind caught the veil and whisked it and the hat off of Sara and blew it away down the road.

"Oh no!" cried Sara to herself. In a matter of a few minutes, her hair was covered by snow and her face was growing numb from the biting wind. *Lord, help me. I'm in trouble, Lord.*

Sara's steps were now hampered by drifts in the road. Several times she stumbled and fell. The third fall she forced herself to get up. She was so cold, so very cold, and so very tired. The day looked like night from the storm. Sara never realized she had dropped the portmanteau in the snow. She trudged through the snow for another twenty feet or so, and then fell to her knees. *Lord, I can't go on. I'm so tired and so sleepy.* Sara sat back on her feet and closed her eyes. *Lord, take me home.* This time Sara did not get up.

CHAPTER FIFTEEN

FOUND

Tennyson pulled the collar of his coat a little higher on his neck. He had his hat jammed down on his head so the wind couldn't blow it away. His hands were fine inside the deerskin gloves, and though his feet were cold, they were not freezing. He knew he would have to brave the freak storm to get to the cabin. At least he knew where he was going and it was only a few more miles before he would reach it.

Suddenly, something flew at the team and blew on by, causing the horses to rear. Tennyson had all he could do to hold onto the team and settle them back down. They didn't like the storm any more than he did. *I wonder what in blue blazes was that black thing that swooped down on us*, pondered a puzzled Tennyson. He finally settled the horses and they kept moving forward. The snow was deepening quickly. The storm was a freak storm, but it was not unusual here in the mountains.

Again the lead horse whinnied and moved to the left. *What in the world is going on?*

Tennyson wondered. As he looked forward, he couldn't see much, but thought he saw something on the side of the road. He halted the team and climbed down from his buckboard. He approached the item which was half-buried in the snow. It was a portmanteau. Tennyson looked all around and called out, but all he heard was the wind as it blew around him. He picked up the bag and put it in the back of the wagon. Someone left the bag behind. Someone could be just ahead and in trouble.

Tennyson hesitated about climbing up onto the wagon seat. If there was someone ahead in the snow, he might not see them or the horses might trample them. He'd better lead the horses for a while and see what lay ahead. Tennyson went to the lead horse and urged the team to move forward. They hadn't traveled too far, when he saw a figure ahead in the road.

As he drew closer, Tennyson thought it looked like someone kneeling on the road. He went closer and realized it was a woman who appeared half-buried, half-frozen in the snow. He spoke to her several times but got no response. He knew he needed to act quickly if she was to survive the storm.

Tennyson led the team past the figure until the tail gate was even with her. Then he grabbed a couple of blankets, that he always carried this time of year, from the front of the buckboard and wrapped them around her. Carefully he pulled her up onto her feet, but when she didn't or couldn't move, he simply picked her up in his arms and swung her up into the bed of the wagon. He put another blanket over her and weighted down the corners so it wouldn't blow off, but would keep the snow and wind off of her. Then he swung up on the wagon seat and picked up the reins. He gave them a snap and called to the team to move forward. They needed to get to the cabin as soon as possible.

The storm continued to blow and snow with intensity as the wagon slowly made it up the road towards the mountains. Tennyson looked back to see if his cargo was still covered and seeing it was so, he turned his attention back to his team, keeping them on the road and moving forward. Finally, the dark silhouette of a grove of pine trees could be seen. Tennyson directed his team for them. As he entered the grove, the wind and the snow lessoned as they were sheltered somewhat. Towards the end of the grove was a cluster of pine and what looked like a log cabin built into the side of a mountain.

Tennyson pulled the team and wagon under the overhang on the barn. Climbing down and unlocking the doors, he carried the woman inside and laid her on some clean straw in one of the stalls. Then he went back out, unhitched the team, and led the horses into the barn. Quickly, he gave them grain and checked to see they had water, then went back out and brought in the portmanteau.

He closed the barn doors, latched them and opened a side door that led directly into the cabin which was actually attached to the barn. He carried the woman inside and put her in a chair by the fireplace. Quickly, Tennyson took his gloves off to light the fire to the kindling and wood that had already been set. Then he unwrapped the lady enough to get to her hands out to inspect them. Holding the small hands in his, he realized they were terribly cold. Stopping long enough to get a pail of water and set it next to the fire to warm, he also filled a kettle with water and set it over the fire to heat. Then back to the lady to undo her shoes and pull off her stockings, inspecting her feet for frostbite and to warm her cold feet with his hands. He kept checking the water as he didn't want it hot, just slightly warm. When he thought it was ready, he poured some of the water into another pan and put it on the floor, then lifted her foot into it a little at a time. He wasn't surprised when she flinched, for he knew even tepid water would feel boiling hot to someone fighting frostbite. Gently, he did the same for the other foot. This was followed by a pan of warm water on her lap and starting the same treatment of her hands.

Tennyson kept adding hotter water to both pans. The fire had caught and was throwing out good heat. The lady's clothes were thawing as well and were damp to the touch. He opened the portmanteau and found a nightgown and put it near the fire to warm it. Carefully and tenderly he began unwrapping the young lady, for he found that she was just that. As modestly as he could, he began to take her things off of her and put the warmed gown on her. Then he sat her back into the chair. He covered her as best he could. Pouring some hot water from the kettle into a cup in which he had added some tea leaves, he carried it over to the lady.

"Miss, you need to drink some of this. I know it won't taste too good, but you need thawing on the inside as well. That's it. Drink a little more. That's a good girl.

"I'm sorry to invade your privacy, but if'n we don't get these things off you, you're not going to make it. I know your hands and feet hurt, but I think they'll be alright, although they may be numb for a spell. I don't know what you were doing out on that road, but it is lucky for you that I found you when I did. Another hour or so and I'm afraid I'd be burying you, not thawing you out. Now you sit here by the warm fire while I fix up a bed here close by."

Tennyson pulled a small bed close to the fire and found some clean blankets to put on it. Then he lifted the gal onto the bed and covered her up as best he could. During the whole time he had been attending her, she had never spoken or opened her eyes. She had started to shiver and he knew the fire and blankets would soon stop that.

"Well, that's all I can do for now. I am going to go back into the barn and check on the animals and bring in the supplies I have in the wagon. You stay here and get warm and rest. I'll be back directly." With that, he went to the side door that led into the barn and slipped through it, closing it behind him.

Where in the world did she come from? I wonder if there is anyone looking for her? Where was she headed? Tennyson shook his head. *Well, she's here now and I've got to care for her. It isn't fit to go back out in this storm. We'll simply have to wait it out.* As quickly as possible, he made trips back and forth to his wagon until he had unloaded his cargo. The food supplies he carried into the cabin then returned to the barn. The rest he stowed away in the barn, and then latched the barn doors again, double bolting them, so the wind couldn't loosen the latch and throw them open.

Returning to the cabin, Tennyson removed his coat and gloves. He checked on the lady. She was not shivering anymore and seemed to be sleeping peacefully. He checked her hands and feet again. There was no sign of frostbite, although they were still pretty red. Tucking them under the blankets, he set about putting some broth on to heat. He then sat down in the rocker near her and the fire.

The trip from town, rescuing the lady and fighting the storm had all taken their toll. The warmth of the fire made him drowsy. *You're not as young as you used to be Tennyson. You feel like a whipped pup. You can relax for a few minutes, then you'll need to get some broth going. This lady will need nourishment when she wakes up.* With that last thought, he tilted his head back and drifted off to sleep.

CHAPTER SIXTEEN
INTRODUCTIONS

Tennyson woke with a jerk. He remembered the events of the night before and of the stranger he had rescued. He sat up quickly in his chair and looked over at the bed.

The young lady was laying there with her eyes wide open, watching this stranger. His face was weathered – the kind that tans easily in the sun. His eyes were green. He was of medium height and build, with hair that was more silver than gray, and even though he was an older man, he had a presence about him that demanded respect. She looked at him with a question in her eyes.

"Howdy, Miss," he spoke gently not wanting to frighten her. "I'm Tennyson. I found you near frozen out on the road leading up into the mountains. I brought you to my cabin as it's the closest shelter for miles. The freak snowstorm has sort of holed us up here for a spell. How are you feeling?"

"I still feel so cold. I think I'll feel cold for the rest of my life."

"That's to be expected, but I think you'll warm up. I don't think you have any frostbitten fingers or toes. They may feel numb for a while though. You sure were cold to hold."

Following that remark, Sara's eyes got bigger. She suddenly realized that she was in bed in a gown, and her clothes were on a chair by the fire. Her face started to redden. "How did I . . . who helped me . . ." she stuttered.

"I'm afraid the only one here is me, Miss. I didn't want to undress you, but your clothes were so wet from the thawing snow on them, I had to do something to get you dry and get you warmed up. I tried not to look any more than was necessary. If it is any consolation, I have two grown children, one of which is a girl," he offered.

"It's okay. I understand. I must have gotten onto the wrong road. I missed the Y where the road splits, I guess. I'm sorry to be a bother to you."

"It's no bother. I'm just glad you're still in good health. I have some broth ready for you. It will help warm you up from the inside out as well as provide you with some nourishment." Tennyson busied himself getting the broth ready which he poured into a cup. Returning to the bed he remarked, "Since your hands are still numb, I'll spoon feed you the broth. May I ask your name?"

"Of course, it's Sara Morrow."

"Hello, Sara. It's nice to put a name to your face."

She smiled as she sipped at the broth he gave her. After finishing most of the broth, she yawned. "I'm still so cold and so sleepy."

"Now you just relax and go back to sleep. Rest is what you need right now. We don't want you coming down with a fever. You rest while I go out and check on my stock and bring in some more wood for the fire."

"Thank you," said Sara sleepily and closed her eyes.

Tennyson pulled on his coat, and went out to the barn to check on the horses. A quick check outside revealed the storm was not letting up. The wind was still howling and the snow swirled around causing deep drifts. *Thank goodness I had cut plenty of wood and thought to stack it in the one stall. I'd hate to go outside in this storm. A man could easily get turned around and lost just a few feet from the door.*

The horses were quiet and seemed glad to be out of the weather, too. Making sure they had hay to eat and plenty of straw, he put a horse blanket on each one to give them a little more warmth. Even though the barn was a lot warmer than outside, it was still cold. Filling their buckets with water completed the task, and Tennyson returned to the cabin with an armload of wood. Laying the wood down near the fireplace, he added a couple of pieces to the fire to keep it going through the night.

Sara seemed to be sleeping peacefully, so Tennyson went to the other bunk, shed his coat and boots, and went to sleep as well.

CHAPTER SEVENTEEN

FEVER

Tennyson got up once in the night and added more wood to the fire. Checking on Sara, he discovered she was awfully warm to the touch. Debating whether or not to wake her to give her more broth, he decided it would be best just to let her sleep. He figured rest was the thing she needed most, and so did he as he returned to his bunk.

The storm outside still did not appear to have blown itself out when Tennyson awoke the next morning. He quietly went to the barn and checked on the horses and fed them. Carrying in some more wood, he built up the fire and put the kettle over the fire to boil some water to make a tea for Sara to drink and some coffee for him.

Sara had not awakened, but was restless as she kept tossing her head and pushing the blankets off of her. Tennyson put his hand on her forehead and grunted when he found her hot. Pulling the covers back up around her, he checked her hands and feet again. They were warm to the touch and no evidence of frostbite. That was a good sign, but he wasn't happy about the fever. The cold wouldn't result in a fever.

As soon as the water boiled, and the tea was ready, he woke Sara. Helping her to sit up, Tennyson encouraged her to drink the tea.

"How are you feeling, Miss Sara?"

"I'm feeling a little lightheaded and confused. Do I know you?"

"I'm Tennyson. We met last night, but you probably don't remember. I found you half-frozen on the road during the snowstorm. I brought you here."

Sara reddened. "I think I'm remembering now. You are the one responsible for my gown I have on."

Tennyson laughed. "Yes, Miss Sara, and may I remind you I have a daughter who is now a wife and mother. I'm old enough to be your father and possibly your grandfather. You needn't be embarrassed that you required some nursing."

"Thank you, Mr. Tennyson," said Sara.

"It's not 'Mr.' Tennyson, it's just Tennyson. My last name is Keye. My mother named me after her favorite poet."

"I see. Tennyson, I'm not feeling too good. My head hurts, and first I'm cold, then hot."

Quickly he felt her forehead again and said, "You're burning up. You need to lie down again. I think you have a fever. But where you picked it up from, I don't know. Being out in the cold shouldn't cause it."

Sara looked up at him and muttered. "There was a little girl on the train. She was hot, too. I was holding her because the baby was fussy, and I told a story and her brother listened, too, and I can't let Jud find me." With that, Sara closed her eyes.

Tennyson tended to her all day. Her fever seemed to climb. He tried to spoon warm broth down her throat, but she couldn't keep anything down. He kept cold cloths on her head, but she fought him over it, complaining about being cold and in the snow. It was all he could do to keep her covered. He went to the back closet and brought out an old flannel shirt of his. Sara had soaked through her gown, so he changed her and the bedding. That was when he made a discovery.

"Well, little mama, we don't dare give you anything that might hurt the baby within you. We'll just have to fight this fever the hard way."

For the next week and a half, Tennyson cared for Sara. He kept her warm, in dry clothing, and even washed clothes out and hung them in the cabin to dry. The storm had finally blown itself out after the fourth day. The snow lay in huge drifts around the cabin. Tennyson kept himself busy with tending to the stock, keeping the wood pile stacked in the event of another storm, and nursing Sara.

Sara had had so little nourishment, that she had lost weight, and Tennyson feared in her weakened condition, that she might die. He constantly tried to get her to take tea or broth whenever she would come to, but in a matter of minutes, she would fall back into a feverish stupor.

A few times, she would speak gibberish about some Jud coming to get her and he would assure her she was safe. Tennyson learned that she had a deep fear of Jud as she pleaded with the Lord to deliver her. He had his own fears. He was afraid that if the fever didn't break soon, he would lose this young mother-to-be before she had a chance to be a mother. *Lord, it's in Your almighty hands. I can't help but believe she is here for a purpose, so guide me that I don't do anything to hurt her.*

CHAPTER EIGHTEEN

DISCOVERIES

After the tenth day of illness, Sara awoke and when Tennyson felt her forehead, she was normal; the fever had broken and was gone. The next week he tended to Sara as she began to eat and gain strength. He even made biscuits and bread as good as any Sara ever made. Sara slept a good deal, but it was a restful sort. She was definitely on the mend.

The snow outside had melted away slowly in the sunshine, with trees dripping with water and the streams gurgling along with added momentum. Tennyson told Sara stories of his family when they first came to the area and Sara listened to the kind man who cared for her so tenderly. She was weak from her fever and depended on Tennyson's help whenever she needed to get up. He was ever attentive to her needs and made her laugh at herself and him in the more awkward times. He assured her not to be embarrassed when he took the chamber pot to empty.

Day by day, Sara gained strength and had more color in her face. She started sitting up, then doing small tasks around the cabin. One morning, when Tennyson returned from the stable, she had breakfast ready. He decided that it was time he talked with Sara about her situation.

"Sara, I need to talk with you so I know what kind of plans need to be made. While you were down with the fever, you did some talking. Most of the time it was just so much gibberish, except for a fear you seem to have for someone called Jud."

Sara hung her head immediately. Of all the people, Tennyson is the one who deserved to know the truth. So she took a long drink of coffee and started. She told him how her mother died when she was young and how her father had raised her and even led her to the Lord. The years of keeping house for the two of them had been idyllic until the accident and her father died.

She explained how she came to live and work for the Haleys. She recalled their treatment of her and about their son. She tried to tell him what happened, but broke down into tears as she related how Jud had forced her in the barn. Then Mrs. Haley's reaction to her pregnancy and wanting to "help" her have the baby and give it up. Sara told had she had run cross country to catch a stage and how she had been on the stage or train for many days until her dream.

She related how she got off at Fulbright, met Betty and Flo, and worked for almost two months. She explained how they had come up with an emergency plan and had to put it into action when Jud showed up looking for her. She also explained how she had gotten off the train at Bloomfield and started walking to the next town when the freak snowstorm had hit. She said she thought she missed the Y turn when she had pulled the veil to the hat down over her face to protect it from the biting snow. After it blew off, the snow kept getting deeper, she kept getting colder, and that's about all she remembered.

When she related how the wind blew her hat away, Tennyson slapped his knee and exclaimed, "That's what flew across the path of my horses! I thought some prehistoric reptile had come back to life!" Sara smiled, for her face had paled while speaking of Jud.

"Well, Sara, it's a good thing your hat blew off when it did. It flew in front of the team and they reared. Of course that slowed us down. Then they were skittish and reacted when they came upon your portmanteau sitting on the road. I had gotten down from the buckboard then, and was walking ahead of the team, because I thought there maybe someone ahead of us in trouble. That's when we found you!"

"I'm so thankful you did. I thought the Lord would just take me then and I'd be rid of Jud forever."

"Speaking of Jud, why is he so determined to find you?"

"He has a fixation in his mind. He thinks he owns me. I guess my reluctance to even be touched by him seems to draw him to me. I thought after he . . . he . . . had his way, he would leave me alone, but if his mother told him I was pregnant, he won't give up anything he thinks belongs to him." She shuddered. "I keep asking the Lord to take away my fear of him, but it always seems to be there, under the surface."

"Well, my dear, you are safe here with me. Hardly anyone knows where this is, and if anyone should come upon us, there is someplace you can hide where they won't find you." Tennyson stood up and extended his hand. "Miss Sara, you need a guided tour of the house here."

Sara looked all around the one room. There were no other doorways, except to the barn, and it was a large single room with stalls and one door outside. This room had a fireplace, off to the left of that was the door that led to the stable, and then the dry sink and cabinets. The wall facing outside had one small window near the dry sink, a front door that was bolted shut, and a set of stacked bunks to the left of the door. Another bunk sat against the third wall with a stand next to it and that brought you back to the first wall with a closet in the corner that you could actually walk into and back to the fireplace. The table and chairs

DISCOVERIES

were in the middle of the room and two rocking chairs in front of the fireplace.

Tennyson watched her as she looked all around. He chuckled at her and said, "Things aren't always what they appear to be. May I?" He offered his hand to her and helped her stand up and led her to the walk-in closet to the right of the fireplace. Even though it was daytime, he stopped by the table near the beds and lit a lantern. Then picking it up, led her towards the back of the closet.

"Sara, this is only used in an emergency. If there are strangers, a fire, or some catastrophe outside, you can come back here and find safety. See here? The back panel behind the hanging clothes can be pushed open and . . ." With a push on the false wall, it opened liked a door and they stepped into a tunnel. Tennyson closed the door behind them and led her down the tunnel deeper into the cave.

"I came upon this tunnel and the resulting caves and came up with the idea of building a home up against the mountain and using the caves as part of it in case of emergencies." After walking another thirty feet, the tunnel opened into a large room. The room had a table and chairs, a double bed, a rocker and padded chair, and extra lamps. "Although it is a little on the cool side, it never gets any colder, nor does it get any hotter. Adjoining this room is the spring room." He led her into the adjoining room and she looked around. To one side she heard the sound of water gurgling. There was a spring and small stream that led from it to the wall where it apparently plunged downward and disappeared.

"Is this where you get the water for the horses and for us?" She asked in wonderment.

"Yes, when the weather is severe. But I also have a well outside the cabin that I use. I use this water only when I can't get outside for whatever the reason may be. This doorway leads from here to the stable room. Come with me." Again he led her through a tunnel. He stopped at one place and said, "Sara, put your hand along the wall and feel." Sara did and discovered there was a notch shaped like an upside down V. "The tunnel that leads to the stable room is notched like that all the way. If your light source goes out, you need to find your way in the dark. The upside down V's means you are headed to the stable. Regular V's on the opposite side, means you're headed to the spring room. There are T's from the closet to the main room and L's means you're headed back to the closet."

"How did you ever come up with such an idea?" exclaimed Sara.

"It was easy, once I lost my light and spent hours finding my way out. I didn't want that to happen twice. Let's go on." A few more feet and Tennyson reached a door. "The doors pull into the tunnels. They won't leave any floor marks that can be seen on the outside. Just make sure you cover your steps into the closet or stable, so they won't lead anyone to the door. The doors can also be bolted from the inside, so if they are discovered, they will be difficult to open." They entered the stable at the back of the storage stall where he kept his feed bins and tack. When he closed the door, he stirred the straw across the doorway so nothing appeared to be disturbed. They were in the barn. "Sara, as you can see, that ends our tour. Let's go back into the cabin. I'm ready for another cup of coffee."

CHAPTER NINETEEN

SUPPLIES

Once they returned to the cabin, Sara poured them both a little more coffee, giving the majority of what was left to Tennyson. She was thinking about the cave rooms and tunnels and reviewing in her mind the markings along the tunnels. She looked up at Tennyson and he was watching her closely.

"Do you have a question, Sara?" he asked.

"If something happens, and I'm in the caves with the doors bolted, how will I know when it's safe to come out?"

"Well, Sara, I can come and get you out. There is another way, but very difficult."

"How long can one stay in the rooms? I know there is water, but what about food?"

"There is a cupboard in the main room with supplies, mostly can goods, in it. I try to replenish it every year and keep it stocked."

"Do you live here year around?"

"No, I don't. I have a cattle ranch about twenty miles southeast of here. I only come

SUPPLIES

up here if I want to hunt or just get away for a spell."

"Are you up here to hunt?"

"No, I wanted to get away for a while."

"Do you need to get back to your ranch?"

"I have a good foreman who runs my ranch while I'm absent. He knows what to do if I'm gone six days or six months. After that, he would come looking for me."

"How long were you planning to stay this trip?" asked Sara hesitantly. She was afraid Tennyson would leave soon and she would need to be on her way.

"Well, as I said, my foreman will take care of things. But I only was thinking of staying a few weeks."

"It's been three weeks already. Do you need to go back, Tennyson?" Sara waited on the answer by catching her breath.

"Sara, you can breathe. I'm not in any hurry to get back to the ranch. However, this leads me to another situation I need to discuss with you."

Sara breathed and quietly waited for him to go on. *Lord, if he needs to go, I know I can trust You to lead me on to the next town and You will protect and keep me all the way, just as You have done.*

"Sara, I only brought a limited amount of supplies with me. I need to go back into town and gather up more supplies in order for us to stay longer. You would be more than welcome to come with me, but I figured you would decline as you don't want to be seen. So I'm suggesting I go in for more supplies, maybe even go on to the ranch and check in with my foreman, and then come back here. That would mean you would be here by yourself for a day or two. Would you be okay with that?"

Sara's eyes lit up at his question. "You mean I don't have to leave? That would be wonderful. I wouldn't need to worry about Jud. The caves are an added safety factor. I wouldn't be afraid to stay here alone, Tennyson. I have felt safer here than any place I've ever lived since I lost my father."

He smiled. "Then I think the first thing in the morning, I'm going to head into town. I'll be gone overnight and will plan to return the following day. If something comes up, I may need an extra day or two, but at the latest, I'll be back by the end of the week. Is there anything you need?"

Sara knew she had no money, so she quickly said, "No, I'm fine."

Tennyson looked at her carefully. "Sara, do you have anything ready at all for this baby?" He knew the answer to his question and he figured she had little or no money to buy anything.

"I don't have anything for the baby," Sara said slowly and automatically her hand went to her stomach. "I guess I need to do that." She looked up at Tennyson with tears in her eyes. "How am I going to provide for this baby? Maybe I should just let Jud find me and do what the Haleys want. At least the child would have a home and food. But I don't want my baby to grow up with them."

"It's alright, Sara. I just thought maybe you would like some material to be sewing up some baby things while you're here. There's not a whole lot of housekeeping that's needs doing. How about I bring you some things to work on to keep you busy. I know my wife would spend the whole winter getting ready for a little one."

"I'll repay you for it – someday. You are so thoughtful, Tennyson. How can I ever repay your kindnesses?"

"Oh, I don't know about that. Let's just say I'm doing it for your father. He sounded like the kind of man who would do that."

Sara smiled from ear to ear. "Yes, he would. I thank you with all of my heart, Tennyson. You're a good man."

"I'm no saint, but I try to live the life He would have me live. So, it's all set. Tomorrow I'll head out. I guess I'd better go check and make sure the wagon and team are ready for the trip." With that, he stood and went to the stable door, putting on his hat and jacket, he tipped his hat to her, and disappeared through the door.

CHAPTER TWENTY

TRAVELING

The next morning, Tennyson left the cabin bright and early. He knew he had a good hour and a half trip in front of him. He was deliberating what he wanted to do about Sara. His heart definitely went out to the girl, and his mind kept going back over her situation and the past few weeks. He didn't think she had a clue of what lay ahead of her with the coming of the baby. How was she going to live, and where? What could she do to keep this Jud from finding her? The best thing would be for her to change her name, and someone take her under their wing.

Tennyson's children were grown, married, and lived elsewhere. He didn't think either Josie or her husband would be willing to open up their home to her. He knew Ned wouldn't, couldn't and shouldn't as his wife was the jealous type. What else could he do? She was too young to come to his place as a housekeeper, especially a single gal with all of the ranch hands around. He shook his head. *Lord,*

TRAVELING

Sara needs someone special looking after her. A thought came to Tennyson, but again he shook his head. Maybe he'd find an answer in town.

When he finally reached town, he stopped at the general store and put in his order with the storekeeper. Tennyson told him he would be by the next day to pick it up. He casually asked if there had been anything going on in town or any strangers.

"Haven't you heard about the three bank robbers who tried to rob the bank. They didn't get away with much, but they did get away. A posse has gone looking for them, but they are not back yet."

"Any other strangers about, besides them?"

"None that I can recall. There was a salesman come in a week ago, but he left."

"Well, thank you for the news."

Tennyson looked around for the owner's wife. He had one other special order to make. He found her rolling up bolts of cloth. He asked her to do up a package of baby materials with needles, ribbon, scissors and thread for a woman to sew on through the winter.

"Your daughter is going to have a baby? You'll be a grandpa again! I'll be glad to put that together for you." She smiled and got started on the order.

Tennyson did not say a word, just turned and left the store. If she wanted to think that it was for his daughter, then he wouldn't argue the point. He wasn't sure he could, even if he wanted to do so.

He decided he would head on out to the ranch and check in with his foreman, Bart. Tennyson spent the rest of the morning on his buckboard and was glad when he finally reached the ranch. A thought kept niggling at the back of his mind. He tried to shake it off, but it kept returning time and again.

As he entered his land, he kept his eyes on the lookout for any problems. Everything appeared well cared for. When he arrived at the house, he went on inside as he knew the men would be out on the spread tending to business. Bart would see his rig and come looking for him when he got back.

Tennyson went upstairs and into the storeroom. He pulled out a trunk and opened it. His heart took a few rapid beats as he looked at familiar clothing that had belonged to his wife. He had thought to give them to his daughter someday, but she was two sizes bigger than her mother, so he simply stored them in the trunk. Sara was about his wife's size. The underclothes and night clothes wouldn't matter as they wouldn't be seen. But he sorted through the skirts and dresses. He didn't want to give to Sara anything that other people would recognize, especially his own children if they saw her. They rarely made the trip home, now that their mother was gone, but one never knew.

Tennyson found some different items that were fairly new and he also thought to throw in some older things Sara could wear as she increased with the baby. He found a smaller trunk and filled it with the things he thought Sara could use and which she desperately needed.

About the time he carried the trunk downstairs, along with a satchel with some of his own things, Bart arrived.

"Howdy, Boss," he greeted, then looking at the trunk and satchel, "Are you fixing on going or staying?" Bart was a tall man with black hair and blue eyes. His face was weathered by the outdoors and he had a ready smile and agreeable disposition.

"I think I'm going to spend the winter in the mountains. Can you handle things at the ranch while I'm gone?"

"Sure, Boss. There isn't too much happening in the winter anyway. I guess it's as good a time as any if you're going to be gone."

"Let's go into the office and go over a few items. I may make the trip back here on occasion if the storms aren't too bad. You know where to find me."

"Yes sir. The only thing that's happened around here is the bank robbery by three men. Sheriff was by, but we haven't seen any trace of them."

"Did he give you a description?" asked Tennyson. "In case they come up towards the cabin, I don't want to entertain a group of thieves."

"They described the leader as a big guy with a buckskin vest and wears a sombrero. The other two were pretty ordinary, except one walked with a slight limp. If I had been them, I would have headed south. This is the wrong time of year to be going to the mountains, unless I already had a place with supplies. Do you think they would head your way?"

Tennyson wrinkled his brow, shoving his hat back a little before pulling it down into place. He sighed. "I don't like to invite trouble, but sometimes trouble just heads your way. Bart, I have a bad feeling about this. I think I may need your help. This is what I want you to do." The two men talked in the office the remainder of the afternoon. Tennyson did not mention Sara to Bart, but he was definitely concerned about her.

"Bart, let's get something to eat and hit the bunks early tonight. I'll head out early in the morning. You head out a few hours later and we'll meet up at the crossroads. That will give me enough time to scout the cabin out. Agreed?"

"It sounds like a good plan, Boss. I'll get the orders out to the men for the day and will head out."

"Thanks, Bart. I'll see you tomorrow."

Bart left the house. Tennyson went into the kitchen and fixed himself some supper and set some things out to take back to the cabin. He boxed everything up and set the box by the trunk and satchel. Then he went into the main room and started a fire to take the chill off the room. He sat looking into flames, praying and thinking. *Lord, give me direction here. I know within my bones, that Sara may be in trouble. Stay with her, Lord, and protect her throughout the night and the day tomorrow. Let no harm come to her. Help me, Lord, to have wisdom and guide my steps. I'll be thanking You for it. Oh, and Lord, help me know what to do about Sara. Amen.*

CHAPTER TWENTY-ONE

VISITORS

Sara found herself a bit sad to lose the company of Tennyson. He had been so kind to her and understanding. She felt safe and protected in his care. But now she was alone, and though she told Tennyson she wasn't afraid, she was.

After he left, she tidied up the cabin. She cleaned and scrubbed everything she saw, not because it needed it, but because she needed to keep busy. She rearranged a few pieces of furniture to give the cabin more room and access to the fire. She went to bed early, and the day's labor helped her fall asleep.

The next day she made sure everything was put away and dishes cleaned and stored. She even cleaned the fireplace and removed the ashes. Midday, she went into the stable and cleaned the horse stalls as best she could and straightened things there as well. She was just about ready to leave when she heard voices coming from outside. She tried to listen and knew there was more than one man. The only thing she knew to do was head for the cave. She didn't dare go back into the cabin as there was a window there. She had cleaned the fireplace, so there wasn't even a fire going, as she had planned to start one on her return. Alright then, she would go to the cave from the stable.

She grabbed the lantern and matches from the shelf over the grain bins, and went to the back of the storage stall. She pushed until the door opened and stepped through. She turned and scattered the straw so there would not appear to be any disturbance. Then she closed the door partway leaving enough light to light the lantern. After it was lit, she closed, and as quietly as she could, bolted the door. Now she needed to go around to the closet door in the cabin and bolt it.

Cautiously she made her way down the tunnel, through the spring room, the main cave room, and into the tunnel leading to the cabin side. Once she got to the closet door, she quietly cracked it open and listened. She heard the sound of glass breaking and someone coming through the window. Quickly, she closed the door and bolted it. She found her heart beating so hard in her chest, that she thought it would jump clean out of it. She picked up the lantern and headed back to the main room. She checked the room out and found the supplies, candles, and matches. Good, she thought to herself. I'll light one candle for now. She did so, blew the light out of the lantern setting it in easy reach of the rocking chair.

She looked in the cupboard and found some canned peaches and crackers. She ate these for her supper thanking the Lord for the food. The water from the spring room was cool and refreshing. She was getting a little chilled, so she pulled on a shawl she had found lying across the back of the rocking chair. Then she sat down in it.

She tilted her head back and slowly rocked back and forth. *Lord, thank You for this safe haven You have given me. Watch over Tennyson on his return that he doesn't run into trouble with these men, whoever they are. Help me to wait patiently for rescue. Amen.* With that said she leaned back in the rocker and listened for any sounds, but only the trickling of the spring room could be heard. After all of the heavy work she had done that day she was tired. After about fifteen minutes, Sara closed her heavily-lidded eyes and fell asleep.

After climbing through the window and unbolting the front door, the man called Country, let the other two men inside the cabin. The biggest man with the buckskin vest, called Red, threw his sombrero on one of the bunks and looked around the room. "Check that door out, Verlyn, and see where it leads." Verlyn limped over to the door and drawing his gun cracked it open, peered inside, then disappeared through the door. In a few minutes he returned with his gun holstered.

"It connects to the stable. I'm gonna unbolt the outside door, so we can put our horses there."

"Good! This is a sweet setup, cabin and barn, all in one. Country, why don't you start a fire? And see about doing something with that window. It's getting cold in here. Verlyn, you tend to the horses and bring our saddlebags in. I'll check and see what kind of supplies they have here."

The three men went about their tasks. Red was disgusted to find the rations were very low, only a few cans of beans and very little coffee. Red looked around the room and checked out the closet to the right of the fireplace.

"It looks like the occupants have left for the winter, or gone into town for more supplies. I hope it's the latter as we will need them." He held up his pistol. "I think I can persuade them to part with them." He guffawed at his joke and re-holstered his gun.

"I'm going to look in the barn for some wood to cover this window," said Country as he went through the side door. He returned shortly with a few boards, hammer and nails and went to work repairing the window.

Verlyn came through the inside door and reported the horses were bedded down. He carried the saddlebags that were across his shoulders to the table and threw them down. "It's getting downright cold outside, the fire feels good. Is there anything to eat?"

Red tossed him several cans of beans. "Open these and have at it."

Verlyn took out his knife and opened the cans. He found a pot and emptied the contents into it and set it near the fire. "Chow will be ready in a few minutes. Is there any coffee?" He looked at Red.

Red pointed to the cupboard and said, "Enough for a pot or two." Verlyn found the coffee and found a coffee pot. He took a bucket and headed outside to find a water source. After ten minutes or so, he returned, set the bucket of water down, and wrapped his arms around his torso.

"It's getting colder out there by the minute. There is a well outside, but it's a cold trip. I'll get some coffee going."

Soon the three men were seated at the table engulfing the beans and slurping down mugs of coffee. The fire cracked in the fireplace and on the whole it seemed peaceful. But appearances can be deceiving.

CHAPTER TWENTY-TWO

PLANS

Tennyson had driven back to Bloomfield early the next morning. He was waiting when the store opened. The supplies he ordered were ready for him and the owner helped load them into his wagon. Even the bundle of baby supplies was stored away under the seat. He made arrangements to have the bill sent to the ranch. Tennyson stretched a canvas over the bed of the wagon, then he climbed up and picked up the reins. With a snap of the reins, he started the team towards the mountains. He was anxious to check on Sara.

As he drove, he prayed. He knew deep inside that Sara was in trouble. Why? Why did he have such strong feelings for this young lady? *Lord, I seek Your direction here. I pray for the well-being and safety of Sara and her baby. Direct her steps, and direct me, Lord. Don't let me do anything displeasing in Your sight. Help me to plan wisely, Lord, and don't let evil triumph. Thank You for Your blessings in my life. Amen.*

When Tennyson reached the turn off, he watched carefully for signs of traffic. Just as he suspected, he came across the tracks of several horses. He knew these weren't the tracks he left behind yesterday, for these tracks covered up the marks left by the wheels of the buckboard and they were headed towards the cabin. Before he was in sight of the cabin, he turned off and went a different direction. After a few hundred feet, he stopped the horses and tied them fast to a tree, and moved ahead on foot.

Climbing up into the rocks, he moved up the mountain. First he came to a crevice in the rock in which he entered sideways, scooting about ten feet in a tight space, but moving nonetheless. Then it opened into a very small chamber in which Tennyson entered. He located a candle and matches and lit the candle to give him light. He crossed the cave and continued down another small tunnel on the left. For the next half hour he worked his way deeper into the mountain, until he found himself entering the spring room. He peeked into the main chamber and sure enough, there sat Sara asleep in the rocker with a lit candle next to her.

Tennyson shook his head. She was so innocent, in spite of what had happened to her, the Lord had graciously saved her from the worst part of it. The only memory she had left was the fear she had of this Jud.

Quietly, Tennyson approached the barred door to the stables and blew out his candle. Without a sound, Tennyson unbarred the door and cracked it open enough to look into the stable. Three strange horses were in the stalls. He opened the door a little more, and looked around. There was no one in the stable. They must be in the cabin as the stable door was barred from the inside. Softly, he crossed the stable to the other side. There was a plaque with a horseshoe on it that he removed. Behind the plaque was a hole that looked into the cabin. Tennyson looked through it to see the three men at the table. The biggest man wore a buckskin vest.

Tennyson replaced the plaque and turned looking around the stalls. He didn't approach the horses as he didn't want them to become restless and whinny and draw the men inside. Instead, he reached into his pocket and pulled out a rolled-up kerchief. Opening it, he exposed several burrs he had picked up back at the ranch. He stuck the burrs on the underside of two of the blankets. Then he took his knife and made a cut into one of the bridles, enough so one good jerk of the reins should cause the rein to snap.

That done, Tennyson went back to the door and entered the tunnel, stopping long enough to stir the straw at the door so his entrance and exit would not be detected. Then he closed and barred the door. Lighting a candle, he returned to the spring room. Sara still slept on peacefully, and Tennyson didn't want to disturb her. He knew she would remain there until he came for her.

He turned and entered the shallow tunnel back to the cave and the rock crevice entrance. Back out in the sunshine, he blinked at the brightness of the day. Going to the buckboard and climbing up on the seat, he waited.

It wasn't half an hour when Bart showed up. With him was the Sheriff.

"Howdy, Boss. Sheriff got back to town about the time I came through, so I invited him to the party. Are the decorations up and everyone here?" asked Bart with a grin.

"Howdy, Bart. Howdy, Sheriff. I'm glad to see you decided to take Bart up on the invitation. I've checked and the guests are here. I've tried to slow any early departure. My, but it is getting a bit chilly out here."

"Yeah, I think we're in for another storm," answered the Sheriff. "Let's get this job done. I won't be happy until I have them all in my jail in town."

The three men discussed the best way to handle the situation. Tennyson wanted to drive the buckboard up to the cabin, but Bart and the Sheriff, though they thought it was a good plan, didn't want Tennyson to be the driver. The men talked a while longer, then the sheriff and Tennyson mounted horses. Bart climbed up on the buckboard and skillfully turned the team around and headed back to the road. The sheriff and Tennyson followed at a distance. Once Bart started up the road to the cabin, the two horsemen split up and approached the cabin from different directions.

CHAPTER TWENTY-THREE
PARTY-TIME

Verlyn sat still listening. Red glared at him for he was talking when Verlyn obviously stopped listening to him.

"Verlyn, what in the world are you doing?"

"I thought I heard a noise coming from the other side."

"I ain't heard a thing, but if you think you did, then git up and go check it out," growled Red.

Verlyn got up and limped over to the side door. He opened it cautiously before entering. Looking all around, he failed to see anything out of the ordinary, so he headed back into the room.

"My ears must be playing tricks on me. I think the wind has picked up a little." He sat down at the table.

"Now that you've satisfied your curiosity, maybe we can get on with our plans. This here is a good set-up for us. It is true that the town we were just in is looking for us, but the next town isn't, especially if there is only one of us going in for supplies. Now, Verlyn, I don't think you were seen very well as you held the horses in the back, so I think you should go into the next town and get us supplies. Although we didn't get all the money we hoped for at the last bank, we got enough for supplies to hold us over."

"Well, if'n you are needin' me to go, I better git as there is a storm brewing," mentioned Verlyn.

"Agreed. So git going. See you in a few hours."

Verlyn got up and went into the stable to saddle his horse. Bridling the horse and then tying it to the stall, he threw the blanket over its back, then the saddle. After cinching the saddle and removing the bar that held the outside door fast, he untied and led the horse outside the stable and closed the door. Stepping up into the saddle, the lone rider started down the road. He had barely gone two hundred yards when he heard a team of horses coming. He jerked on the reins to stop and turn his horse into the brush when the rein on the bridle snapped loose. His horse reared and pitched its rider into the brush before running off on down the road.

Sheriff Dunston had not gone far when he heard a horse approaching. The rider-less horse appeared and he blocked its progress, catching it by one of the reins. He moved on ahead and saw Bart's wagon, but no Bart. Before reaching the wagon, Bart came out of the brush prodding a man who was limping along.

"I guess someone decided to leave the party before it got started," commented the Sheriff.

"Not soon enough," replied Bart. "His horse dumped him when the rein snapped.

"Well, let's get him spruced up with a rope and we'll leave him here while we go on. You tie his hands and I'll get his feet."

"You're not going to leave me here in the freezing cold, are you?" whined Verlyn.

The Sheriff grunted, "You were already out in it. A few minutes won't kill you."

"But I had my horse to keep me warm. The ground will send the cold straight to my bones!" complained Verlyn.

"Well, Sheriff," remarked Bart, "he has a point. Why don't we tie him up to this tree and let him hug it."

"Good idea. Only I best stuff this kerchief in his mouth, so his tongue doesn't freeze or give away our position."

After Verlyn was trussed up and tied to the tree and his horse securely tied to another one, Bart climbed back up on the buckboard, the sheriff remounted his horse, and they continued on with the plan.

Tennyson had gone back to the rock face and reentered the crevice opening to the caves. He quickly moved through the tunnels. Checking on the sleeping Sara, he continued on to the stable. This time when he looked into the stable, one horse was missing, and the stable door was no longer barred. One of the robbers was missing. That meant they only had to deal with the two that were left.

Tennyson quietly entered the room and grabbed a rope. He tied it across the doorway at ankle level. *That should slow them up a little.* He looked around for something else. His eyes lighted on some locks hanging in the storage stall. Taking them down, he went to the doors of the stalls for the horses. He deftly slid the locks in place and locked them, then replaced the bar on the outside door. *I need something else to slow down the departure of the party-goers.*

No noise came from the cabin. Tennyson looked through the hole under the plaque. Two men sat at the table talking. Sounds outside of a team driving up, brought both men to their feet. Tennyson quickly replaced the plaque and headed back into the tunnel. He bolted the door shut in the darkness, not taking time to light a candle. He headed down the tunnel following the marks on the wall. Coming to the spring room, he tiptoed past Sara and entered the other tunnel. Again he followed the carvings on the wall to find his way to the closet door. Unbolting it, he cracked it a little and peered out. He could see nothing, but he could hear the two men discussing the approaching wagon.

The bigger man said, "You go through the stable and come up on him from that side. I'll get him from the back. No, wait. He stopped. He's just sitting there looking at the cabin. The smoke – I bet he sees our smoke from the fireplace. He's getting down – now he's waving at someone. Country, I think it's a setup. Let's get the horses saddled and get out of here.

PARTY-TIME

The two men grabbed the saddlebags and raced for the side door. Country went through first, caught the rope with his foot and pitched forward to the floor. Red was right behind him, hollering for him to get out of the way, when his foot caught the rope and he stumbled forward.

"What in tarnation was that? Who put that rope there? Look around, Country, someone must be in here." Red drew his gun and started looking around.

"Red, someone has locked the stall doors shut, but I don't find anyone. The only person that was in here was Verlyn."

"Wait 'til I git a hold of him. I'll have his throat for this!

"Red – look! Someone has barred the doors shut from the inside. Verlyn couldn't have done that, could he?"

"Something weird is going on. Let's get out of here. Bust the stall doors open." Red took his booted foot and kicked at the door until the wood splintered. He led his horse out and started to saddle it. Country had more trouble getting his door opened, but he finally did and got his horse out and started saddling it. Red unbolted the door and threw it open. He led his horse out with Country following close behind. Both scurried to mount their horses. As soon as their backsides hit the saddle, Red shouted, "Let's ride!" and both horses began bucking.

Red and Country held on for dear life while the horses bucked and kicked and finally pitched their riders off onto the ground.

Country fell on his arm wrong and the "snap" sounded in the air as well as his scream of pain. Red landed hard himself, but without mishap, except when he started to rise, his face met the barrel end of a shotgun. He started to reach for his gun when the man said, "Try it and it will be the last thing you do this side of glory." Red just hung his head.

Through the doors of the stable, Tennyson came through with his pistol drawn in one hand and a couple of ropes in the other. He tied both men up. There they sat until the Sheriff came up. Red was glowering and Country was whimpering from the pain.

"Well, boys," said the Sheriff, "it looks like the party is over. Bart, can you catch their horses? I'd hate to make them walk the whole way back to Bloomfield."

"Sure, Sheriff, they haven't gone far, though what got into them to make them buck so is a mystery to me," replied Bart as he left to catch the two horses belonging to the robbers. When he brought them back Tennyson spoke up.

"You'd buck, too, if someone sat on you with a couple of burrs between you and the saddle," grinned Tennyson as he reached under the blankets and removed the burrs he had planted.

Tennyson disappeared while the two men were deposited on their horses with their hands tied behind them. Country was in agony with the pain, but the sheriff showed him no pity. The sheriff took the saddlebags and threw them across his saddle-horn.

"Where did Tennyson go?" asked the sheriff.

"I don't know. Maybe he left to get my horse from wherever he left him. He'll be back shortly, I'm sure."

"I hope so. It's going to storm again and I want to get these hombres back in jail before the storm hits."

Soon Tennyson reappeared riding Bart's horse.

"Here's your horse, Bart." said Tennyson.

"Well, Bart and I will pick up the third one we treed and head back to town." Sheriff Dunston settled in his saddle and said, "Tennyson, we can't thank you enough for finding these scoundrels and inviting us to the party. We will see you the next time you're in town."

Bart tipped his hat and said, "Have a good rest, Boss. We'll see you in a few weeks?"

Tennyson smiled, "Not sure when, Bart, but I'll let you know. Of course, as cold as it is, we could be headed for some bad weather. If I get snowed in, don't worry."

"No problem, sir."

With that, Bart mounted his horse and he led the cavalcade down the road. The sheriff brought up the rear with the robbers between them.

Snowflakes started to fall. Tennyson walked down the road to the parked wagon and his team. He climbed aboard the seat, released the brake and drove the horses up to the barn. By the time he had unhitched and settled the horses in their stalls, the snow was coming down in earnest. He started unloading the supplies inside the barn, then barred the door. He removed the rope from the doorway, and carried the things that belonged in the cabin inside.

Tennyson built the fire up. Everything looked back in order, except for the broken window and it had been boarded shut. It was time to get Sara out of the cave. Tennyson found a lantern and lit it. He went through the closet and headed down the tunnel to the main room and Sara. He saw no light coming from the main room. He quickened his step only to find the room emptied. No Sara, no light. He looked up to the spring room in time to see her step through the doorway. When she saw Tennyson, she flew across the room into his arms and hugged him.

"Tennyson, I was so scared when you left. Then these three men broke into the cabin through the window, so I came back here and I've been waiting for you to return," she chattered in relief at seeing him.

"It's all okay, now. The men are gone for good. It's just you and me. Wait here for a moment as I unbar the tunnel door to the stable, then we'll return to the cabin."

Quickly, Tennyson went down the tunnel, removed the bar, and returned to the main room. "Let's go. I'm getting awfully hungry, aren't you?"

Sara smiled and nodded.

CHAPTER TWENTY-FOUR
SNOWBOUND

That night the snowstorm hit with full force. By morning a gale was blowing and drifts several feet high were thrown against the cabin. It was hard to tell daytime from nighttime as the sun was never seen through the dark storm clouds overhead.

Tennyson busied himself outside by dragging a couple of logs into the stable area where he could cut them up and stack them for firewood. He knew the area well enough to know that it could be weeks before they could get out.

Sara busied herself by putting away the supplies and becoming acquainted with all that they now had. Tennyson had instructed her to keep a running list of things they needed so if another trip was made, they wouldn't be overlooked. When Sara came across the bundle with all of the baby material, ribbons, needle and thread, she sat down in her chair and cried. God had led such a Godly man to intercede and help her.

Tennyson found her crying in her chair. He quickly put down the load of wood he was carrying, and asked her what was wrong. Sara looked up at Tennyson and said, "I was just thanking the Lord for providing such a special man to find me and care for me. You have rescued me twice and even now, I am thankful for the protection you give me in this place. I have come to love it and treasure the time we've had here."

"Sara, we have got to do something about you. We shouldn't be here alone, now that you have recovered. As soon as this storm passes, we need to return to town."

Sara fell to weeping at this point. The thought of Jud finding her filled her with such fear and dread. "Couldn't I just live here alone? Oh, Tennyson, when I return to town, I'll be doomed. I might as well give up and give in – Jud wins. I'll live the rest of my life fearing him and what he can do. I don't think I could do that."

"Sara!" Tennyson spoke her name sharply. "That is no way to think. You have to trust in the Lord to guide and provide for you. The Lord has a solution for you. We just need to find it."

"What solution can that be? I can't work, and that's even going to be more so as I get bigger."

Tennyson scratched the back of his head. *Lord, lead me. This thought keeps coming back to me, but it doesn't make a whole lot of sense. Is it really what You want? Please direct our steps.* He gently took Sara's chin in his hand and lifted her face so he could look into her eyes.

"Sara, there is only one way I can think of, that will insure your protection from Jud and provide you and the baby with the thing you need the most – a different name. You need to be married to someone who will provide for you and take care of you. A husband will give the baby a name and watch out for you," he hesitated for a second and went on. "Sara, I want you to consider letting me be that husband. I know I'm old enough to be your grandfather, but I can give you my name and am well able to care for you and the baby."

Sara's eyes opened wide. "Tennyson – you would do that for me? You would give up your freedom to care for me and take my baby on and raise it as your child?"

"I would. But the arrangement doesn't seem fair to you. You're young and your life is before you. You could meet someone someday that you truly love . . ."

"Tennyson! I already love you for who you are and what you have done for me. I would never betray or leave you. You have my promise that if I become your wife, I will be faithful and honor our vows. We would be married in every sense of the word. My answer is I would be honored to be your wife. I only have one request."

"What's that?" queried Tennyson.

"That we spend the winter here in the mountain cabin. In the spring, I will go wherever you want me to go, but for this winter, I want to be here."

"I suppose we can do that. As soon as this storm breaks, we'll go into town and get married. Then we'll come back out here. We'll need to get whatever will be needed for the rest of the winter as we might not get another chance."

"I agree." Sara stood, smiled and gave him a peck on his cheek. "Thank you, Tennyson, for more than you will ever know."

CHAPTER TWENTY-FIVE

WEDDING

The storm blew itself out after three days. It took another two days of sunshine to melt it enough that the wagon could be used. Though the road was muddy, Tennyson thought it could be navigated and he didn't want to get caught in another storm.

During the days they were kept inside, Tennyson asked Sara what she wanted in her wedding. Did she want a church wedding or one by a Justice of the Peace?

Sara said the Justice of the Peace was fine. They worked on a list together of things they wanted for the winter. Tennyson showed Sara the trunk he brought and she was delighted with the clothes. She told him she never had more than a skirt, a dress and two blouses at a time, and those were hand-me-downs.

Sara was so elated. For the first time in her life since she went to live with the Haleys, Sara felt that she didn't have to be constantly on watch for fear of Jud. She knew Tennyson was much older than Jud, but Tennyson was a man that could take care of himself and her. She knew he had a ranch, but she didn't care about it so much. The cabin in the mountain seemed like home and probably always would. She knew that a marriage to an older man may mean she would someday need to care for him, but she would do it gladly for what he had done and was doing for her.

The following day, they drove into Bloomfield. For the first time, Sara was going to a town without fear of Jud. She felt safe with Tennyson seated next to her. Sara was excited at the thought that she would not return as Sara Morrow, but as Sara Keye and her little one would bear the same name. Determined that Tennyson would never regret his decision, she prayed, *Lord, bless this man who has rescued me from the storm, from robbers, and now from Jud. Help me to be a true wife to him and ever make me faithful to this man.*

Tennyson told her he would drop her off at the store first. She could turn in the order for supplies and look around for anything that might take her fancy. Sara looked at him as though he had two heads.

He laughed, "Consider it a wedding gift."

"I don't need or want a gift. Your name is the most precious gift anyone has ever given me. I couldn't ask for more."

"Well, you look anyway. Pick up some doodad that catches your eye and add it onto the order. I'll come by and pick you up. We'll have our noon meal at the hotel's restaurant, then go to the Justice of the Peace, and afterward, pick up our order before we head back to the cabin."

When they reached town, Tennyson dropped her off at the general store as he promised. She went in with her list and looked around at all the wonderful things they had. When the storekeeper's wife asked if she could help her, Sara said yes, she had a list that needed to be filled. She would pick it up after the noon hour if that would be alright with her, which it was.

Sara looked around the store at all of the wonderful gadgets and doodads on display. She didn't find anything fancy, but she did find an eight-day clock that was simple, but very attractive. She thought it would be nice to have at the cabin, and it was something both of them could enjoy. She added it to the order.

About that time, Tennyson came through the door and spoke to the storekeeper. Quickly, Sara walked over to him and they left, before anyone had a chance to question them. Who was the young lady with Tennyson? When did she come to town? Questions were asked, but there was no one who had any information.

Tennyson had had his own problems. The Justice was an old friend and a retired judge, Judge Samuel Lawson. He had tried to talk Tennyson out of the marriage. He said any girl wanting to marry a man as old as Tennyson must be a gold-digger and would take Tennyson for all he was worth. Tennyson told him he wasn't going to argue the point that Sara wasn't like that. In the end, Sam reluctantly agreed to do the ceremony that afternoon. Tennyson asked him not to tell anyone about it until the spring of next year. They would be gone, so there wouldn't really be any need for anyone to know until they returned. When Sam asked why, Tennyson just responded that he had his reasons and to let it go at that.

Tennyson and Sara went to eat at the restaurant. Sara told him she had so many butterflies going around in her stomach, that she wasn't sure she could eat anything. Tennyson laughed and asked her if she was sure it was butterflies. Sara looked at him with a strange look on her face until she realized he meant the baby. She blushed and said she hadn't even thought about that. Maybe that was the feeling she had in her stomach – baby, not butterflies.

After ordering, Tennyson turned serious. "Sara," Sara sat up to listen. "Sara, I told you I had two grown children. Josie and Ned are good people, but they are not going to understand you and me together. You also are going to pose a threat to their inheritance."

"No, Tennyson!" interjected Sara. "I will not do that to your children. You are providing me with your name, and if I never get a single nickel from you, you have been generous and kind, and I'll be fine as well. I will not ask for more. I don't want to interfere in any way to cause a break between you and your children and grandchildren."

"It still won't be easy. The day will come when they meet you and see you are more a younger sister than a stepmother. You also know, Sara, this is a small town and people will gossip. I'm afraid I can't protect you from that."

"I was prepared for people to talk about me anyway. A single woman expecting a baby – you are not saving me from anything that I wasn't going to have to face, no matter where I went. But you are giving this child your name. That is enough. I love you for that, Tennyson."

Tennyson smiled. Just then the food was served and both of them ate quietly, lost in their thoughts of what would lie ahead for them. They took their time over dessert and coffee. Tennyson wanted Sara to have a good day to remember.

When they left the restaurant, Tennyson suggested they check about a new dress for Sara.

"No! Please, no! You have given me so many new things. I have more clothes than I know what to do with."

"There weren't any new dresses in that trunk. I think you should have a new one to be married in at least."

"No, Tennyson, no new dress. I have a 'new' dress on and I am pleased to be married in it." Sara suddenly had a thought. "Maybe this is a dress that your wife wore and it brings back memories. I'm sorry, I never thought."

"Don't give it a second thought, Sara. It was a new one my wife bought and seldom wore. It looks very pretty on you."

"Thank you, Tennyson."

"Well, then, let's go visit the Judge." He took her by the elbow and helped her cross the street and go down to the Judge's house at the end of the street. Tennyson explained that he and Samuel Lawson were old friends. The Lawson house was the second from the very end. It was painted white with green trim.

When Tennyson and Sara entered the house, and he introduced her to Judge Lawson, the Judge widened his eyes. Then he turned and gave Tennyson a questioning look. Tennyson wrinkled his brow and gave his head a small shake.

Sara saw the interchange and broke in on the silent argument. "Judge, I know I am younger than Tennyson, a lot younger, but I'm sincere when I say I love and care for him and will honor my marriage vows as long as we both shall live."

"I'm sorry, Miss, if I have offended you. I just care about this old coot as well. If you both are certain that this is what you want to do, then we'll get on with this wedding. My wife, Karen, will be a witness." He turned and called to his wife, "Karen, will you come to the parlor, please."

Karen emerged from the kitchen and was introduced. The Judge read the vows and Tennyson and Sara repeated them. In a matter of minutes, the ceremony was concluded and the license signed and witnessed. Both of the Lawsons congratulated both of them, and Mr. and Mrs. Keye left to walk back into town.

Tennyson had left his wagon in front of the store and had told them inside to have it loaded. As soon as they arrived back at the general store, Tennyson helped Sara onto the buckboard seat and excused himself long enough to go inside and make arrangements for the bill. He also took the time to write a note to his foreman, explaining the additional supplies were to be paid. He would be staying at the cabin until spring. With that finished, he rejoined Sara. Pulling a blanket up around her, for the air was getting colder by the minute, Tennyson untied the reins and called to the team. The newlyweds were on their way, leaving a puzzled storekeeper, a worried judge, and otherwise ignorant town of the change in the lives of the couple driving out of town. But one young lady sat with a song in her heart, all fears gone, and a smile on her face.

"May I ask why the big smile?" questioned Tennyson.

"I'm smiling because I have been rescued once again by my hero! This is the third time you have rescued me. I am whole, I am safe, and now I am free, thanks to you, Tennyson, and I love you for it – now and forever!"

"That long, eh?" he said with a grin.

"Maybe even longer," was her answer.

CHAPTER TWENTY-SIX

HONEYMOON

When Tennyson and Sara headed back to the cabin, the snow kept coming down faster and faster. Tennyson pushed the team in order to get home sooner. When they arrived at the barn entrance, Tennyson unhitched the horses while Sara started carrying supplies inside. The sacks of grain she left for Tennyson, but everything else was unloaded into the barn from the wagon. As he started carrying the grain, Sara carried the cabin supplies through the door and began sorting and putting them away.

The wind outside started to howl and Sara busied herself getting the fire started and getting some coffee and a stew going over the fire. Tennyson came through the door and spoke briefly.

"I'm going out to pull some logs into the entrance of the barn. I can cut them up in there. This looks like it could be a bad storm and I don't want us to grow low on wood. I have some logs at the far end of the stable. I'll drag those in. It should be enough."

"Do you need help?" asked Sara.

"No, I'll use one of the horses if I need to do so. Are you all set in here?"

"I need some water, but I can get that from the spring cave."

"I would rather you wait and let me get it. I must get the logs in first before the weather is any worse. Why don't you just work on putting supplies away."

"I can do it. I'll be careful. You be careful outside."

Tennyson went back out. Sara picked up the bucket. She could do this. She started back to the closet when she remembered she would need a lantern. She stopped, lit a lantern, and carrying it and the bucket, started back through the tunnel. She filled the bucket and picked up it and the lantern, heading back. The bucket was heavy. She should not have filled it up, but she didn't want to make too many trips. Part way through the tunnel, she had to turn sideways to get both the lantern and bucket through. She suddenly felt a severe stitch in her side and a pain shot up her back. She set the lantern and bucket down and waited for the pain to go away. She rubbed her stomach and took several deep breaths. The pain eased up so she picked up the lantern and bucket to continue on down the tunnel. Back inside the cabin, she set them down and sat for a few minutes until the pain was gone completely.

Rising again, Sara continued making coffee and set it on the fire to boil. Then she started cutting up some meat and potatoes to cook for a stew. As she worked on supper, she took time to make biscuits and started them baking. She occasionally felt a cramp, but ignored it as she kept working. She was determined to have the supplies put away before Tennyson came in for the night.

The wind outside howled and she wondered how Tennyson was doing. She went to the side door and opened it. There was no sign of him; however there were several logs on the floor. The air in the stable was cold. Sara went to the barn door and looked out. All she could see was the blinding snow and the terrible wind. She called out for Tennyson, but her words simply flew back in her face. Now she was worried. What if he got turned around, or had fallen or hurt himself. *Lord, look after Tennyson. Keep him safe while he is outside and help him to do his work without harm. Watch over us in this storm, I pray. Amen.*

No sooner had she finished praying, when she heard a noise coming towards her. She opened the door in time for Tennyson and the horse to drag in another log. As soon as they were inside, Tennyson helped her close the door against the wind and he bolted it from the inside.

"What are you doing out in the cold without a cloak?" inquired Tennyson.

"I was looking for you."

"You need me for something?"

"No, I was just concerned. I thought you might have been in trouble."

"Well, I'm fine. Now get back in the cabin. I'll be in as soon as I get the horse settled in and fed."

Sara turned and did his bidding. She checked on her biscuits to find them done. The coffee was hot, but the stew was far from done. She cut several strips of bacon and put them in an iron skillet to fry. By the time Tennyson made it back into the cabin, she had everything ready.

Tennyson took off his outside coat and hung it and his hat on the peg. He set his gloves by the bench and took off his outside boots. He put on another pair of boots that were dry and set the wet pair near the fire.

"I have coffee ready with biscuits and bacon."

"It sounds good to me. Do I smell stew?"

"Yes, but it won't be ready until tomorrow."

"The bacon and biscuits will do me fine. It looks like you have put all the supplies away. You aren't doing too much, are you?"

Sara hesitated only a moment before replying, "No, I'm fine." She quickly went to the table and set the biscuits on. Then she gathered the strips of bacon on another plate and set them on the table. She poured coffee for both of them and looked up. "Everything is ready."

Tennyson came to the table and sat down. He held out his hand for hers, bowed his head and thanked the Lord for His provision and His protection from the storm. He also thanked Him for Sara and the baby, and asked Him to give both good health. He asked the Lord to bless their marriage as well. After he said *Amen,* he looked at Sara.

"I am thankful for you. I do want you to be happy."

"I am, Tennyson, I am." Just then Sara took in a quick breath. Another pain shot through her back and she instinctively held her breath and waited for it to pass.

"Sara, what is it?" asked Tennyson urgently.

"A pain . . . in my side . . . and back. It's starting to ease up." She took a few deep breaths and then sighed. "That's better. I must have overdone. I'm fine now."

Tennyson had a frown on his face. "No more work for you today. I think you had just better rest."

Sara agreed. "I think I'll go lie down on the bed for a few minutes. You go ahead and eat. I'll be fine." She got up from the table and started across the room when she doubled over in pain. "TENNYSON!" she cried.

Jumping from his seat, Tennyson caught her before she went down. He picked her up and carried her to her bed. Sara looked up at him with frightened eyes.

"Something's wrong. I can feel it. It's my fault. I did too much, but I wanted so much to please you." The pain came on again and Sara cried out.

Tennyson prayed again. *Lord, we're in need here. Something is dreadfully wrong. Help us to do what is needful. Let no harm come to Sara. Help this pain to go away. Guide us, Father. Use me to help her. Amen.* Once again Sara cried out in pain. Tennyson knew the signs. The baby was coming three months too soon!

CHAPTER TWENTY-SEVEN
GOOD-BYES

Tennyson sat staring into the fire. He had done all that he could, but it wasn't enough. The baby didn't survive. Sara lost quite a bit of blood, but the bleeding stopped and she was resting. He had wrapped the wee thing in a blanket Sara had made for it, and let Sara hold it for a few minutes. Though premature, it looked perfect, though so tiny. Sara touched its face with her fingertips and gently kissed it on the forehead. Then he laid it in one of the boxes that they had gotten supplies in and tended to Sara. He held her for an hour while she wept in his arms for her loss; wept until she was completely exhausted. He spoke soothing words to her assuring her it was not her fault until she finally fell asleep. Even then she whimpered as she slept.

The wind was still howling outdoors. The snow had deepened and the cabin and barn were barely visible from outside. There was another storm brewing inside the man who sat staring into the fire. After all the doubts and misgivings, Tennyson had been sure the marriage was what God wanted. He had returned from the wedding feeling sure it was the right thing. Now, after only being married a matter of hours, the baby was gone. The surety he felt was gone. The reason for Sara's flight and fear was gone. The hope of a future was gone. Sighing, he stirred the fire and added another log. The biscuits and bacon and coffee were cold. It was how Tennyson felt inside.

If he could get her back into town tonight, he was sure the judge would dissolve the marriage and Sara would be free. But with this storm, that possibility was gone. This storm would probably last through half of November. Other storms were sure to follow here in the mountains. They would be lucky to get out again this year, let alone this week.

He looked over at the bed. Sara slept on. She was exhausted by the labor, the loss of blood, and the weeping. She would probably sleep through the night. Tennyson knew he needed to tend to the baby. He picked up the box with its precious contents and carried it out the side door. In the barn, he went to the tunnel door and set the box down. He lit a lantern and pushed the door ajar. He picked up the box and carried it inside and down the length of the tunnel. At the spring room, he crossed over to the opening to the back tunnel and continued his journey to the small cave by the crevice opening. There he set the box off to one side in a small alcove. He gathered stones to stack in front of the alcove to hide the box until spring and the thaw came. Then he would bury the baby outside once the earth had softened again.

"Little one, rest here until spring. I'll come for you then and I promise to do right by you as well as your ma. I'm proud that you will bear my name on your tombstone. I only wish I could have known the boy you would have been." *Lord, our little boy is with You now. I tried to do right by him and his ma, but You must have had more need of him in heaven with You. Please let him know he is loved. Help Sara to come to terms with his death and not blame herself for being the cause. Show me what we should do now.* With that he retraced his steps back to the spring room, but instead of going on, he turned and entered the main room and sat down on one of the chairs. He felt like an old man tonight. Then he bent his head into his hands and wept as he hadn't wept since his wife died. The silence of the caves kept the weeping from being heard by anyone except the One who created them. And who can say whether the dripping sounds heard, came from the spring room or from a higher realm.

Finally, Tennyson stopped, stood, and after retracing his steps back to the stable, blew out the light, and closed the door. With tears still in his eyes, Tennyson picked up the ax and started chopping on one of the logs. All night long, the steady *chunk, chunk, chunk* of the ax could be heard as he worked through most of the night, stopping only long enough to stoke the fire and check on Sara. In the early hours of the morning, he went into the cabin and lay down on one of the other bunks and fell asleep.

CHAPTER TWENTY-EIGHT

HEALING

The first week after Sara lost the baby, she slowly gained her strength back. She had lost her appetite and hardly ate anything. Tennyson was very attentive but distant. Sara couldn't blame him. She felt like she had trapped him into a marriage and now the reason was gone. He had agreed to raise the baby as his own, give him his name, but it had been all for nothing. Never once had he accused her of causing the premature labor, but she accused herself. It was her stubbornness about getting the water that started the problem. She should have waited for Tennyson like he asked. No, she had to do it her way.

The cabin was silent and charged with emotion. Neither Tennyson nor Sara spoke what was in their heart. Tennyson felt he should give Sara time to heal, but the wound wasn't healing. If anything, it was festering. She wasn't eating enough to keep a bird alive and her eyes had dark circles under them. He should have fetched the water for her on the spot. Because

HEALING

he wanted to pull the logs in first, she felt she had to do it. It was his fault the baby died. Finally, he could stand it no more and he went back to the cave room to pray.

Lord, we are in a bad way here. Sara is hurting and she is starting to look sickly. I am worried she will give up on living and die right before my eyes. It wasn't her fault. I failed her. Forgive me, Lord. Now she needs help. How can I help her, Lord? I can't. I don't know what I should do. Only You can help us.

Sitting in the darkness with the prayer going through his mind, he waited for an answer. How long he sat, Tennyson had no idea for he knew he could not rush God. Trusting that the answer would come, Tennyson sat quietly and waited.

Suddenly, with a start, Tennyson sat up. He must have dozed off, but an idea, actually a simple thought, came to his mind. No problem could ever be fixed unless it was brought to the surface. He needed to talk with Sara – really talk. They were both avoiding the root of the problem between them. He headed back to the stable and on into the cabin. Sara was at the sink peeling potatoes.

"Sara, we need to talk. I think we need to sort out what is going on here. Come sit by the fire, please, and talk with me."

Sara quietly moved to the rocker and sat down. She turned her brown eyes on Tennyson and then looked away. She was anxious about what he was going to say.

"Sara, I'm so sorry about the baby. I don't want you to blame yourself, it wasn't your fault. If it is anyone's fault, it is mine. What I am concerned about is that now you are trapped in this marriage with me. If we had known about the loss of the baby, you could now be free to move on with your life."

"Be free? Move on with my life? Tennyson, it was my stubbornness in going against what you asked that is to blame, not you. *You* are the one that is trapped. You agreed to give my baby your name – now he is gone and you are stuck with me. You are the one who should be free."

"Sara, I don't feel stuck. I didn't offer to marry you just for the baby. But now you have no reason to be married. Jud won't bother you now that the baby is gone."

"Not bother me? I don't even know if Jud knew about the baby. He would come after me regardless. Tennyson, I need you more than ever." She dropped on her knees before him and with tears running down her cheeks, she looked up at him. "More than ever, Tennyson, I need you more than ever, but I thought I had ruined it for us."

Tennyson lifted her up off her knees and onto his lap. She was such a frail little thing. He held her head against his chest and spoke softly. "I need you as well. You've given me a purpose again for living. When I first found you, I was on my way up here to decide what to do. My life had no meaning anymore and my children no longer needed me. I was just going through the motions. Then I found this ice maiden who desperately needed me and I haven't once regretted it. It's just that our ages are so far apart. I worry that you will regret being tied to an old man."

Sara sat up. "To me, you're not an old man, you're my hero. What does age have to do with that? Tennyson, do you still want to be married to me?"

"If that is what you want, then I do."

Sara laid her head on his shoulder again. They sat there for the longest time. Then very quietly, Tennyson spoke again.

"Sara, one last thing, we need to come up with a name for our son. We'll want to put it on the tombstone in the spring. What was your father's name?"

"Mathias. Mathias Morrow."

"Does Mathias Keye suit you?"

"How about Mathias T Keye for a name? You and I will know what the 'T' stands for in his name."

"Thank you, Sara. I would like that for my son."

"I like it, too."

"You know, Christmas will be here in about six weeks. What do you want for Christmas?"

"Want? Tennyson, I have what I want. To be here with you, safe and secure."

"There must be something."

Sara thought for a few seconds and said, "I wish the window was fixed. I get awfully tired of not being able to see outside. I know we're surrounded by snow, but I still like to look out."

"Hmmm. I bought a new piece of glass, but with the last storm, I haven't thought about trying to put it in. If tomorrow is fair, I'll try to do so. I'm just glad the robbers took the time to board it up so we had protection from the storms."

"I want our first Christmas to be special. But then, sharing it here with you does make it special."

"Well, we'll see what we can do."

"Tennyson," began Sara.

"Hmmm," responded Tennyson.

"If you'll let me up, I'll finish peeling potatoes and will fix us some supper. I am hungry, all of a sudden," she admitted.

"That sounds good to me. I'll tend to the stock and then be back in for the night."

Both got up to do their separate tasks with lighter hearts and smiles on their faces. The healing had begun and they could move on now as one.

CHAPTER TWENTY-NINE

CHRISTMAS

The closer Christmas came, the more secrets played a part in the routine of the cabin dwellers. Tennyson spent a great deal of time in the stable area working on a special project. Sara worked inside crocheting a scarf and gloves for Tennyson as well as trying to plan special treats for the Christmas dinner. The kitchen area once again had a glass window in it, which added light and a view that Sara enjoyed.

Two weeks before, Tennyson had gone hunting and brought home a deer. He took care of dressing it out and cutting the meat up for Sara. They packed the meat in a small crevice in the outside wall where Tennyson had built a door to close it off from animals. The freezing cold weather kept the meat longer. Some of it Sara had dried, and the rest she had used in stews, roasts and such. Tennyson worked on curing the hide in hopes of making Sara a pair of moccasins and a warm cape for the colder weather of the mountains.

Sara had enough material to sew Tennyson a new shirt and several handkerchiefs. She also retrieved the clock from where she had stored it and wrapped it as well. Both of them became even busier as Christmas Day approached. They sat at the supper table grinning at each other as they contemplated the surprises they had in store for the other. Both of them wanted this Christmas to be one they would remember.

Christmas Eve day, Tennyson went hunting again and came home with a turkey. Both of them worked on getting it ready for roasting. Sara saved the feathers in a sack so as not to be wasteful. She worked on her baking so the next day the oven to the side of the fireplace would be available for roasting the turkey. She made bread, cinnamon rolls, cookies and pies. She reigned in the kitchen with her wooden spoon as her scepter which she also used to banish Tennyson from the area when he tried to taste some of the treats.

At mid-afternoon, Tennyson hauled in a pine tree he had set on crossed boards to stand in the middle of the room. Together, they made garlands of popcorn, hung small bows of ribbon, and topped the tree with a star Tennyson fashioned out of tin.

After supper on Christmas Eve, Tennyson read the second chapter of Luke in the Bible. Sara made them hot sassafras tea to drink and set a plate of cookies down to munch on while they enjoyed the fire and the tree. Sara sang all the Christmas songs she could remember and Tennyson joined her with his deep baritone voice in the choruses.

Sara sat on the floor leaning against his knee. He reached out and touched her hair and stroked it tenderly. She was his girl now, and he intended to watch out for her.

Sara sat there thinking how thankful she was to be here, safe from Jud, safe with Tennyson, and surprisingly, happy. *Lord, thank You for the blessings You have given me. Thank You for Tennyson and for the care and kindnesses he showers on me. Help me, Lord, to be a good wife to him. In Jesus' name, I pray. Amen.*

Sara smiled up at Tennyson. She was ready and her heart overflowed with caring for this silver-haired man who was her rescuer, her hero.

The next morning began with another snowstorm outside, but inside the cabin was sunshine and warmth. Tennyson quickly went out to tend to the horses for the day and even gave them extra grain as it was Christmas. The turkey had gone into the oven in the early hours of the morning and its aroma filled the air.

Sara cooked potatoes, noodles and green beans to go with the turkey as well as the baked goods from the day before. She set the table with a candle in the middle and hummed as she made preparations.

LESSONS OF HONOR

Several packages made their appearance under the tree as the morning went on. Sara was most excited about the one big one Tennyson brought in that was hidden under a horse blanket. She had suggested she look at it right away, so the horse could have his blanket returned, but Tennyson said no, it was an extra one and didn't need to be returned right away.

Finally the time came for Christmas dinner. Tennyson prayed and asked God's blessings on the day, the week ahead and the new year to come. After the *Amen,* they both enjoyed the good food before them and each other's company.

Following dinner, they opened the gifts they had for each other. Tennyson liked the new gloves, scarf and cap Sara had made for him. He was pleased with the shirt as well. Sara was fascinated with the moccasins he had made her and swore she never would wear shoes again. The cape and mittens he had fashioned for her were also admired. Sara tried them on and then couldn't put them down; she was so busy petting the softness of them. She let out a squeal of delight when Tennyson uncovered a free standing quilt rack for blankets. He had made it with pine cones carved into the sides as decorations.

Tennyson was equally pleased with the clock she had picked out on their wedding day. Using his pocket watch, he set it and wound it up, setting it on the mantle over the fireplace where it could be seen and admired.

"It's been a wonderful Christmas, Tennyson," remarked Sara. "The best one I have ever had in my life. Thank you, Tennyson, for everything – for being here with me – for being my hero – for being my husband. I mean that in every sense of the word."

"Sara, this has been a Christmas to remember. Unlike any I have had before. I am proud to be your husband." With that, he gathered her into his arms for a blessed Christmas in a small cabin, in the mountains, in the winter. A Christmas blessed by God himself to such an unlikely couple, at least, not since Boaz and Ruth as recorded in the Old Testament.

CHAPTER THIRTY

WINTER

*S*ara and Tennyson kept busy throughout the wintry days of being snowed in. First of all, there was the matter of simply taking care of day to day tasks, like fixing food, cleaning stalls, taking care of wastes, hauling water, keeping clothes and people clean. It kept them busy in the mornings and early afternoons. Then Tennyson came up with an old checkers game in which they both were very adept at playing and that kept the evenings lively. Tennyson also found some books that they read together along with the Bible as they sat and enjoyed the warmth of the fire.

Not long after the New Year, Tennyson took on a project to make a double bed from two single bunks. Using some planks from the stable area, he fashioned a frame and once the frame was completed, he drilled holes through all of the side boards in which to string rope to hold a mattress.

Sara kept busy making one mattress out of two single mattresses as well as sewing two blankets together to make one large blanket. She actually did that twice as one blanket was not enough for the cold winter nights. They were both pleased with the result of their efforts as they worked together at making their little cabin snug and comfortable.

It was towards the end of February that Sara started getting sick in the mornings. She was usually a little better by mid-afternoon, so she knew what the cause of the nausea was. By the second week of March she was better, and she knew she needed to tell Tennyson.

March brought with it some soft weather. The snow melted and water was running everywhere. Sara took walks along the road breathing in the spring air of the mountains. It was as if spring suddenly appeared and flowers broke out all over the mountain. She loved it up here. She could easily continue to live up here, although she knew her time in the mountains was growing to a close. Tennyson was talking about the ranch and she knew he needed to get back to it. He said there was another bad storm headed their way. He brought in more wood and filled the wood stall once more. Supplies were getting low, but there still was enough to make it through to the time of their departure.

The break in the weather also gave them another opportunity. Tennyson dug a small grave and carried the box out to it. Sara and Tennyson together bade their little son good-bye again and buried him in the mountains where he was born. Tennyson had made a wooden cross with the babe's name and date on it. "We'll get a regular headstone for him and bring it back so it will last a long time." Sara agreed and said she would plant some flowers then. For now, she laid some spring flowers she had picked for the occasion on the tiny grave.

Sara asked Tennyson if he wanted to leave for the ranch now, but he said there was still much to do to get the cabin ready to vacate and he didn't know if the weather would hold out that long. He told Sara all that needed to be done in the cabin. She went to work cleaning, and making a list of anything that needed to be brought to the cabin on a permanent basis. Then she started packing things she would take with her. She really didn't have much, but there was more than she expected.

Sara got out the baby materials and started sewing again during the evening. About the third night, Tennyson stepped over and picked up the baby blanket she was working on.

"You feel you need to make this up just because we have it?" he asked.

"I'm in no hurry, if that is what you mean. After all, we've got until late August or early September before they will be necessary."

"Is that sodi-water?" replied Tennyson as he went back to his chair and sat down.

He sat there for a moment when he suddenly stood up again and looked at Sara. "Are you meaning to say that you're with child?" he asked in amazement.

"Is that so hard to believe? I suppose now you are going to accuse me of seeing another man?" She remarked smartly.

"Not hardly. Really, Sara, a baby? Our own?"

"Our own. I figure it is a late Christmas present and it's all yours."

"Well!" Tennyson walked back and forth in front of the fireplace. "After all these years," he grinned, "I didn't know I still had it in me."

"It would appear so. So what do you want, a boy or a girl?"

He came to her then and squatted down beside her. "All I want is a healthy baby and mother. That's what I want. And I will cherish both of them, whatever God gives."

"Thank you, Tennyson. Now git up off your knees or you won't be able to walk tomorrow."

"Yes, ma'am."

He went back to his chair with a grin on his whiskery face. He sat there in thought then Sara noticed a change. Something was on his mind.

"Sara, how soon can you be ready to leave for the ranch?" questioned a worried father.

"I thought we weren't going until after the next storm comes through. Have you changed your mind?" asked Sara.

"I'd feel better if you were closer to town where we can get a doctor for you if there is any problem. And I want to start looking for a housekeeper so you won't overdo while you're carrying."

"And what shall I do? Sit around and drink tea while a hired woman works rings around me? I'm not made of glass. And I won't be so foolish as to carry something I know is too heavy for me." Sara replied indignantly. "I won't be mottle-coddled!"

"I don't want to take any chances. If anything should happen to you or the baby, it would be more than I could bear. You mean too much to me, Sara."

Sara sighed. "You mean so much to me as well, Tennyson. And I'll do whatever you say. But I doubt I could sit around doing nothing, so leave me something to do."

"I promise, my dear, I promise." Tennyson paused for a few minutes, and then said, "So how soon could you be ready? This nice weather won't last more than a few more days, I'd say."

"Let's see, how about the day after tomorrow. I can be ready by then if there's no big hurry. I can be ready tomorrow if there is a hurry."

"Let's head out about noon tomorrow. We'll stop overnight in town. That way I can leave my list of supplies at the store and have them ready to load the day after and we'll head to the ranch the next morning. I am warning you, I have little supplies left at the ranch house, so don't worry if your list is long. Write down anything that you can think of you might need for cooking and such."

"I'd better start on my list tonight then, if I'm to have it ready that soon. I think I will leave my cape and gloves here as well as my blanket stand. That way they will be here when we return."

"What about your moccasins?" he asked with a grin.

She stuck one moccasined foot out in front of her and grinned back at him. "You know I won't part with these moccasins. If they get to looking too worn out at the ranch, then you'll just have to make me a new pair."

"I think I have created a real problem here all in the name of a Christmas present. What about the clock? Shall we leave it here?"

"No. I want to take it with us."

"I think we should, too. Well, Mrs. Keye, we will soon be approaching your new home at the ranch."

"Promise me, Tennyson."

"Promise you what, my dear?"

"Promise me that you will bring me back to the cabin. I love it so."

"I see no reason why we can't come back. You need to see it in the summertime and autumn. Each season is special in the mountains. Don't worry, Sara, I'll bring you back." promised Tennyson. "I'll see you come back to the mountains you love."

CHAPTER THIRTY-ONE

BLOOMFIELD

The next morning was a busy one as Sara and Tennyson packed the buckboard and tried to leave the cabin and barn in good shape. Tennyson made sure there was wood laid in the fireplace in case the next time the cabin was used, a fire was needed quickly.

By noon they were both ready. Sara looked back at the log cabin and barn that she had called home for the last several months. They had been good months except for the loss of Mathias, and she had gotten to know Tennyson's heart, his faith and his way of thinking. She glanced at this husband of hers. Though his hair and mustache were silver, bordering on white, he was still agile and strong, although Sara knew there were times his arthritis made him feel differently. Sara herself felt safe in his company and happy to be seen with him.

The day was a beautiful spring day for the drive to Bloomfield. Tennyson laughed and told her a little of when he first came to the area and worked at the ranch. A lifetime of hard work and blessings from God had resulted in the ranch he had today. Sara asked him to describe the ranch, but Tennyson said she would have to wait and see it for herself. Sara told him it didn't matter what the ranch looked like or what shape it was in, as long as they were together, she would be contented.

They reached Bloomfield by mid-afternoon and Tennyson first drove to the hotel. He arranged for them to have a room, signed the book and got Sara settled. Then he said he would run some errands, drop the list off at the general store and see to boarding the horses at the livery. He would be back in time to take her down for supper. In the meantime, he suggested she may just want to rest. He started to leave when he turned around and came back into the room.

"Sara, the millinery and dress shop is just two doors down from the hotel. Why don't you go have a look? Maybe you might find a new dress and bonnet to wear. And maybe a new pair of shoes, since you can't wear your moccasins forever." he added.

"I could do that, but how would I pay for them?" she asked.

"Tell them to bill Tennyson Keye's ranch. Everyone here knows I'm good for any debts." He turned and went out the door.

Sara sat and looked around the room for a few minutes. It didn't take long for her to decide to take him up on his offer and go look for a new dress. She put on her cape and checked her reflection in the mirror. Her clothes were not new or fashionable, but they were clean and serviceable. She sighed, they weren't very pretty. With a shrug, she headed out the door on her excursion in town.

Tennyson made a quick stop at the store and gave his order. He told them he would have his buckboard brought around in the morning for loading. He then went to the livery and made arrangements for his horses and for someone to hitch and drive the buckboard over to the store the next morning. Everywhere he went; he was greeted and nodded his head to different ones he knew.

After he finished at the livery, he walked down the street stopping at the office of J.W. Drew, Attorney at Law. Spending an hour and a half there, he came out feeling that it had been a good day. He had one quick visit he needed to make with the Judge, so he headed in that direction.

Sara had gone into the dress shop and was delighted with some of the dresses she saw. There was one dress in particular, with small pink roses on the skirt and sleeves with a bodice of a solid rose hue. After measuring and fitting, Sara decided to get it. The only alteration was the hem and the dressmaker said it would be ready in two hours. Sara asked if it could be delivered to the hotel and made arrangements to do that and where to send the bill. She next went into the millinery shop and found a straw hat with pink rosebuds on it that she thought would match the dress. She asked if it could be delivered to the hotel and they agreed it could. Everyone was so nice, especially once she told them to send the bill to Tennyson's ranch.

As luck would have it, she did not find any shoes as comfortable as her moccasins, but she did find a pair that fit. She ordered those and asked for delivery as well. Then she went back to the hotel feeling very scandalous at what she had done. If it had been too much, then she would return every item, but he had told her to look for a dress, bonnet and shoes.

She quickly took advantage of her time alone and had a good sponge bath. She thought she could order a bath, but she was new to the hotel world and simply made good use of the pitcher of water she had in the room. When they got to the ranch house, she would get a good bath and wash her hair.

She was done with her ablutions when a knock sounded on her door. When she opened it, she found her orders had arrived. She quickly took the items and set them on the bed. Then on a spur of the moment, she changed into the new dress, bonnet and shoes. She had just looked into the mirror to see her reflection when Tennyson arrived.

He whistled low and smiled. "I see I'm going to need to change into some better duds if I am to escort this beautiful young lady to the ball."

"Oh Tennyson, don't be silly. I have probably spent way too much money and I should just take these back so they don't cost you."

"No you won't. I like them and I want you to keep them – especially the shoes – I don't want my wife walking around town in her moccasins." He grinned.

She returned the grin. "Then you had better get changed in a hurry. I'm hungry, and lest you forget, I'm eating for two!"

"Yes ma'am. I will change quickly and no, I will not forget. Give me about fifteen minutes and we'll go downstairs and give Bloomfield something to talk about, for Mrs. Keye, you are going to make a sensation on this town."

So they did.

All through dinner, Sara was aware eyes were upon her and Tennyson. He simply told her to ignore them, and pretend they were eating together back at the cabin.

"I think not, Tennyson. We didn't have fancy plates and glasses and silverware at the cabin. And the cuisine was certainly not the same," she whispered.

"No, I liked yours better. But this will keep us from starving, don't you think?" he took another bite and added, "You may not realize it, but I really married you for your cooking. I look forward to what you can make on the stove at the ranch house."

"Probably just a mess. But I'm not sure that in my delicate condition I should be lifting those heavy pots and pans and iron skillets."

"Don't worry, my dear, I'll hire someone to do just that for you so you can cook."

"I think it would have been easier to simply have hired a good cook and have done with it."

"True, but a hired cook doesn't come with all of the extra amenities." He lifted an eyebrow as he said it.

Sara almost choked on the sip of water she had taken. Tennyson could be so ornery at times. "If you cause this cook to choke to death, you won't have a cook or any extra amenities. Tennyson, I'm finished. Dinner was delicious and we are full. What's next on your agenda this evening?"

"How about a quick stroll about town and then we'll call it a day and retire to our room. Tomorrow is already a full day, and I can hardly wait for you to see the ranch."

"I'm all for that." She waited as he helped her out of her chair, and gave her his arm to leave the hotel and walk through the town. They hadn't gone far when Sara shivered.

"There, you are cold. I should have gotten your cape. I'm afraid our spring weather won't last much longer. It looks like another storm will hit before the end of the week."

"We still have time to get back to the cabin," suggested Sara.

"It's mighty tempting, but I think we'd better not. We'll be better off at the ranch for right now. But I promise you, we'll go back some day." Turning her around, they walked back into the hotel and up to their room.

Little did they know the rumors had already started their rounds. Instead they went to bed and enjoyed a good night's rest in spite of what was being said.

CHAPTER THIRTY-TWO

JUD

The next morning, Tennyson and Sara went downstairs to the hotel's restaurant for breakfast. While they ate, he laid out the plans he had for the day. After breakfast, he would let her pack up their things while he finished a couple of errands. Then he would pick up the supplies and buckboard at the store and come back to the hotel to pick her up before they left for the ranch.

Sara was agreeable, so she packed things up while he was gone and left the bags by the door for the porter to carry them downstairs. Tennyson left the hotel and went straight to the office of J.W. Drew. From there he made a trip to see the Judge once more, then he headed for the general store.

The buckboard was loaded and Tennyson stopped in long enough to talk with the storekeeper before he drove away. He arrived at the hotel, loaded the bags Sara had packed and helped Sara up on the seat. They were starting through town when a shout was heard. "Sara! Sara Morrow!"

Tennyson felt Sara stiffen beside of him. He pulled the horses to a stop as a blonde young man approached the wagon.

"Sara! Finally, I have caught up with you. You thought you could give me the slip, but I've found you. I've hunted for months trying to follow your trail. I told you you could never hide from me. You might as well face facts and come back with me now." His tone was loud and furious. People were starting to pay attention to the drama.

"Jud, it is too late," started Sara. "I will not come back with you. I want nothing to do with you or your family. Now leave me alone and go away!"

"I won't go away until you come with me," Jud said and started to move toward her.

As the conversation had been going on, Tennyson had quietly slipped off the wagon seat and walked around behind it coming up on Jud from that side. Just as Jud reached up to grab Sara and pull her down, Tennyson quickly pulled his gun and had it in Jud's face.

"Excuse me, young fellow, but you are causing an unnecessary disturbance in our otherwise peaceful town." As Tennyson spoke with the gun in Jud's face, Jud was backing up more and more until he found himself pinned against the end of the horse trough.

"The young lady, has no desire to go with you, so you best cool off and leave her alone."

Jud set his jaw as he faced the old man. "Old man, I don't know who you think you are, but . . ."

Tennyson jabbed him in the chest with his gun. "Let me tell you who I am. I am the official husband of that young lady and have been for the last five months. I expect you to honor that and you are to leave her alone." He jabbed him again. "And if I ever see you around her again, I may just forget what an honorable man I am and get rid of scum like you."

Jud still refused to believe Tennyson's words. "I can't believe she would marry the likes of you when she could have someone like me."

"Son, I think you'd better get over yourself and cool off." With that, Tennyson took one last step toward Jud which threw him off balance and he fell into the trough. Jud came up sputtering.

About that time, the sheriff arrived and asked Tennyson if there was a problem.

"No sir, Sheriff. This young man was just getting cleaned up for his trip out of town. But if I see this young pup again, there will a problem." Tennyson turned to Jud one more time, "You see, son, when you get to be an old man like me, you just get tired of putting up with vermin. So you just shoot them. After all, how long can they lock a body up when they're old? If they hang me, that's alright, too. I've lived a long full life and going to my Maker a little early doesn't make much difference to an *old man!*" Tennyson walked back around to his side, jumped up on the buckboard seat and called to his team to, "Step up!"

They pulled away from the buzzing crowd and drove on out of town. They had traveled about a mile when Tennyson stopped the team and turned to Sara.

"Sara, are you alright?" he asked with concern.

Her face was pale and her breathing erratic. She was trembling. She seemed almost paralyzed by her fear.

"T-Tennyson," she stuttered, "you've saved me again. I *knew* he would find me. I *knew* it."

"Yes, but it didn't get him much. He found me instead. He won't be back to bother you. I think he realized it is now a hopeless situation."

"Would you really kill him, Tennyson?" Sara asked.

"Me? That was just all bluff," reassured Tennyson. "I have to admit it, though, I even convinced myself that I would do it." He laughed a little, when suddenly Sara broke into tears and leaned against Tennyson for support.

"I have been so scared for so long," she said. "Just seeing him brought it all back. I'm sorry I'm such a weakling."

"A weakling? My wife? The one who sat there and told him she didn't want him and to go away? You hid your fears pretty well if you ask me. Now dry those tears. The worst has happened, Jud didn't win, and you can live your life once more without him hanging over your head."

Sara sniffed and dabbed her eyes with the handkerchief he offered her.

"Let's go home, Tennyson. I'm ready."

"Step on," called Tennyson and the buckboard moved forward once more.

CHAPTER THIRTY-THREE

RANCH HOUSE

Bart sat on his horse on a high hill overlooking the ranch. Sitting with the ease of a man long since used to spending long hours in the saddle, he relaxed under the brim of his cowboy hat gazing over the scene below him. His blue eyes squinted making small wrinkles at the corners of them. His thick black wavy hair was subdued for now under his hat and he sported a two week old beard that framed his face. He was lean from hours of hard work and athletic in his demeanor.

Bart had worked for Tenn for the last twelve years. He started as a young teen that was willing to learn and be taught by the best and Tennyson Keye was just that. Bart grew into a young man who was trustworthy and loyal, not afraid of hard work, nor of giving his very best.

Bart sniffed the air. There was a storm coming on soon, maybe even tonight. The ranch was ready for it. He had the men check all four corners of the place the last few days to make sure the herd had come through the winter without problems. They had.

The sound of a wagon drew his attention to the far west side of the spread. Sure enough, there was a buckboard and it looked like the boss himself was driving it. Bart picked up the reins that had been resting on the saddle-horn and clicked with his tongue and cheek to his horse. "Let's go, Sampson, Boss will expect to see us at the house." A slight indication of the reins and horse and rider turned and headed down the slope.

Tennyson drove the team around the bottom of the high hill, but came to a stop when the ranch came into view in the valley slightly below them. Sara gasped at what she saw. There was no barn with a log home beside it. This was a big ranch. A large barn with several outbuildings and four large corrals, a bunkhouse with a cook shack next to it, and the ranch house. It wasn't any simple log home; it was a two story, clapboard house with shutters, a wrap-around porch, and stone steps that led down to the drive. There was an area for a large garden behind it and what looked like an herb garden with a statue in the midst of it. There were large old oak trees around the perimeter of the house and one in a side yard that sported a swing. The porch was wide and looked so inviting, begging for someone to stop and sit a spell.

Sara's eyes widened in amazement. "Tennyson, this is all yours? This is your ranch house?"

"Yes ma'am. It sure enough is. Do you think you can make it a home, Sara?" He looked into her eyes and saw the surprise and wonder in them. "Are you surprised?"

"If I had come upon a castle of stone with a moat and dragons, I wouldn't be more surprised. Tennyson, it is too wonderful for words. Make it a home? I'll try, but Tennyson, there is one problem."

"A problem?" he frowned. "What's that?"

"If you expect me to fill that home with children, you'd better plan on living until you're 110!" she looked at him. "Three of us could get lost in there!"

"Oh, come on now. It isn't that big. The porch makes it look bigger than it truly is. I just hope you'll feel at home."

"If you're there, I will. But Tennyson, I still love our mountain home best."

"I understand. It has some real special meaning for me as well, and our son rests there." He smiled and started the wagon forward.

As Tennyson helped Sara down from the wagon, he told her just to go on up into the house and explore. He would bring the luggage and supplies up, or have one of the men to help him. Sara started up the steps and had just slipped inside the front door when Bart rode up to Tennyson.

"Howdy, Boss. I thought it was you on the wagon."

"I thought that was you up on the hill, as well. Bart, I'm home and I have someone special with me this trip."

"I saw you had someone in the wagon with you. A relative?"

"Yes, in a way, a wife. Bart, I got married right after we caught those robbers last fall. We spent the winter together in the cabin as Sara loves the mountains. But I felt it was time we came home here to the ranch."

"Boss, congratulations!" said Bart as he heartily shook Tenn's hand. "It's a bit unexpected for us, but I guess it's no longer that way for you."

"No, it isn't. Sara is a good woman, but she's had some rough times behind her. Bart, I need you and the men to know, she is young, very young. I know how that sounds for an old coot like me, but there it is. Why don't you grab an armload of supplies and come on up and meet her."

Bart and Tenn gathered up as much as they could carry and climbed the steps to the kitchen door. They deposited everything on the table when they heard light footsteps coming down the hall.

"Tennyson, it's wonderful!" exclaimed Sara as she burst into the kitchen, then came to a standstill at the sight of a stranger. She stared at the tall man whose thick black hair fell down into his face as he removed his hat and whose blue eyes widened at the sight of her.

"I knew you would like it. Sara, I want you to meet my foreman, Bart Rogers. Bart, this is my wife, Sara."

Bart looked at Sara in a stupor. The glow that lit her face was one he would never forget. Those big brown eyes that made you feel weak-kneed kept him tongue-tied for a few uncomfortable seconds. Then he came to himself and stuttered out a "Glad to meet you, Miss, or I mean, Ma'am."

She smiled at him and said thank you. Tennyson broke in with the suggestion that he and Bart should bring up the rest of the supplies. Sara should start putting things away so she knew what she had in the cupboards. Bart and Tenn both left to return to the wagon.

After the supplies were all brought up to the house, Tenn asked Bart to tend to the horses and wagon, then come back up to the office and catch him up to date with what was going on with the ranch.

Bart said, "Sure, Boss." Then turning to Sara, he added, "It was nice to meet you. Welcome to Keye Ranch." Then he escaped out the door to the team and wagon below.

"Tennyson," Sara said as she stood directly in front of him. "You never told me how well off you were. I feel like I am such an imposter to live in a home like this. It is so big and beautiful."

"Not to worry, Sara. You'll get used to it. At least we know you didn't marry me for my money."

"No, I married you for being my hero," she smiled a little and added, "who owned the cabin in the mountains."

CHAPTER THIRTY-FOUR

BART

Bart climbed onto the buckboard, flipped the reins and called to the team, "Step up!" As he drove them to the barn he shook his head. He wasn't surprised that the Boss married again, but to marry a mere girl, a third of his age. And what is in this marriage for her, but his money.

Bart mulled the whole idea over in his mind while he brushed and curried the horses after feeding them. Boss was the most honorable man he knew. Maybe she trapped him in some way and the only honorable thing to do was to marry the girl. He thought it kept coming back to the ranch and wealth. She must be money hungry to marry an old man like that. Of course, she didn't *appear* to be that way. Looks could be deceiving, though, Bart had to admit.

He walked on over to the cook's shack where the men were gathered for dinner. He'd be expected to tell them of the latest development. He made the announcement and the room became so quiet that you could hear the soup bubbling on the stove.

"Married? What's she like, Bart?" asked Toby, the youngest of the group.

"Well, that's the thing. She's young."

"How young is young?" This time Rafferty spoke up.

"Very young. About eighteen or nineteen." Bart grimaced. Someone whistled.

"When did he get married?" Toby spoke again.

"I guess about five months ago. Anyway, that's all I know about it. I have to go back up and report to Boss in the office. I just wanted to fill you all in on the news."

Bart turned and started for the door.

"Is she pretty?" *Toby and his questions* thought Bart.

"Yeah! She's pretty." Bart muttered without turning around. He simply went on through the door to report to Boss.

Bart and Tenn went over the books and Bart gave him the latest tally on the herd.

"I had the men bring the cows with calves and the ones that are due to drop theirs soon, in to the large corrals at the barn. I think they will be easier to feed if we do get a bad storm, and we won't lose as many new calves as we might if they were out on the range."

"Well, Bart, you did well while I was gone. I knew you would. I'm thanking you and will reflect that a little better in your next paycheck."

Sara appeared in the doorway.

"Tennyson, dinner is ready." She turned and headed back to the kitchen.

"Why don't you join us for dinner, Bart?"

"Why, thank you, sir. That would be great, but I'm headed into town. I want to go and get back before the snow comes on again."

"Yep. I thought it felt like snow might be coming at us tonight. Well, don't stay too long and get caught in a squall. I can't afford to lose my best foreman."

"Right, Boss. I'll watch out for it. Have a good evening and welcome home again," replied Bart as he shook hands then left, heading to the barn to saddle up Sampson.

On the ride into town, Bart hunkered down inside his coat. The air was definitely turning colder. This would be a quick trip, although exactly why he was going, Bart didn't know. He didn't want to eat with the Boss and his wife, but he didn't want to face the men again and all the questions and comments that he would hear. This whole marriage business had truly thrown him for a loop.

Bart got into town and headed for the local restaurant that catered to cattlemen. He ordered, but found he wasn't all that hungry when the food came. He heard a couple of men talking about the events earlier in the day involving Tenn and his new wife. As he listened to the talk, Bart had to grin to himself as he pictured Tenn backing the culprit into the horse trough with his pistol. But he dropped the grin when he heard the comments about

Tenn and his new bride – something about Grandpa robbing the cradle.

Bart suddenly realized he was finished, although his food wasn't even half eaten. He paid his tab and walked out before any more was said, or someone realized he was sitting there. Bart didn't want any trouble, but for some reason he felt like it wouldn't take much to start trouble.

As he walked out of the restaurant, he felt snow bite against his face. He looked up to see the flakes swirling down from the night sky. He'd better just head back to the ranch before he was caught by the storm. He had an uncomfortable feeling this storm could be a bad one and he should be back with the men.

Bart untied Sampson's reins and stepped up into the cold saddle. He shivered as a sharp gust of wind blew past him. Coming into town had been a bad idea. He didn't feel any better, only worse. Now if he could only figure out why Boss's marriage bothered him so. Well, time would tell, he expected. Time would tell.

Bart pulled his hat brim down a little lower and headed Sampson out of town in the direction of the ranch. Bart had a long, lonely and cold ride ahead of him.

CHAPTER THIRTY-FIVE

STORM

The storm came with a terrible force that night. Snowdrifts were everywhere as the cold blustering wind whistled through every crevice it could find before slipping off to blow elsewhere. Bart was thankful he made it home last night before the worst of it had hit. His decision to bring the cows with calves and cows ready to birth into the corral was a smart one. They could get skids of hay out to the cattle to feed on and the barn offered shelter from the worst of the storm. Hopefully, this will be one storm without terrible problems.

Bart was in the barn when he heard the door to the barn open. He didn't pay it much mind as he figured one of the ranch hands had entered for something. Then he heard a desperate cry.

"Bart! Bart! Where are you? Help me! It's Tennyson. Come quick!" Sara, with only a small cape over her shoulders had trudged through the snow to the barn. As quickly as she arrived, she disappeared.

Bart immediately went to the door and could barely make her out as she trudged back through the snow and drifts to the house. Something was terribly wrong. Bart followed behind her fighting the wind every step of the way. It was amazing how Sara, as tiny as she was, could stand against the gale and not be swept off her feet. The thought no sooner crossed his mind when she went down face first into the snow. Quick as a wink, she scampered back up on her feet and plunged ahead like a woman possessed to get back into the house.

When Bart reached the back door, there was no one in sight. The cape laid on the floor and soaked shoes had been cast off to the side. He went through the door into the hallway. He called out only to be answered by a voice upstairs. Bart shed his coat, hat, gloves and boots by the back door and started up the stairs.

Sara met him in the hall. Her face showed traces of tears and her anxiety was obvious. "It's Tennyson. He wasn't feeling well last night when we went to bed, but it was nothing specific. This morning he complained of being cold, but when I checked his forehead, he was burning up. I've tried to get some nourishment in him, but he isn't responding to me."

"Carolyn, I'm so cold," muttered Tennyson in a feverish whisper.

"He's been calling for Carolyn," explained Sara.

"She was his wife for forty-two years," remarked Bart.

"I know. I didn't mean that it upset me; it's just that the fever has him out of his mind. Otherwise, he wouldn't be talking as if Carolyn were still alive." Sara spoke woodenly, sensing Bart didn't approve of her. But that didn't matter. What mattered was getting Tennyson well again. "He needs a doctor."

"I'm afraid that won't happen soon enough to help him. The storm has shut down all chances of getting out on the roads. Carolyn used to have a tonic for fevers and such that she kept in a cupboard in the kitchen. I don't know what was in it, or if there is any of it left, but it's about the only thing I know to do for him. I'll go and look to see if I can find it."

"I saw some medicines in the cupboard left of the dry sink. Try there first. I'll try to keep him sponged to keep the fever down."

Bart hurried downstairs and looked in the cupboard Sara mentioned. Sure enough, he found a bottle of the elixir on the second shelf in the very back. He looked until he found a glass and spoon and carried them back upstairs.

Just as he was about to enter the door, he stopped to see Sara kneeling before Tennyson. She was begging God to spare her hero and not to take him home yet. Bart watched as tears rolled down her face. Bart felt he was intruding, so he cleared his voice and walked on into the room.

"I found the tonic. I'm not sure what's in it or how much to give him. I think she used to thin it some with water." He handed the medicine bottle to Sara. She quickly swiped her face with her hands and took the bottle. She looked at the outside of it and took off the cork and smelled it.

"It smells like a mixture of herbs. It says 2 tablespoons per dose, every two hours. It looks a little thick to me. We'll thin it down with some water. You'll have to help me by sitting him up."

Bart lifted him up and held him in an upright position. Sara deftly mixed the solution and water and then tried to get Tennyson to drink it. He took a little, but not enough of it to satisfy.

Sara told Bart to ease him back a little as she was going to try something. As Bart eased him back she took one hand and pinched Tennyson's nose shut and as soon as he opened his mouth, she started pouring the medicine down his throat. He sputtered and choked, then settled.

"You can lay him down again. We'll need to do this again in a couple of hours. If you need to be with the men, I'll understand as long as you come back and help me with the next dose."

"I'll be glad to do so, although it didn't look like you need too much help. That is kind of a dirty trick to play on a man."

Sara smiled a little. "I have had to nurse someone who was a terrible patient and wouldn't take medicine. It was the only thing that worked." Her face became serious once again. "I only hope the tonic helps. He doesn't complain of pain, nor are any of his limbs paralyzed. It's the fever. He's so hot. I'm almost half-tempted to put him out in the snow. At least it would bring the fever down."

"That seems a little extreme to me. What if I bring a bucket of snow in for you to put your wet cloths in to help cool him?"

"That's a great idea, Bart. I'll try anything to keep him alive and get him over this. I thought it might be the flu, but so far, his stomach has not been upset."

"I'll go get that bucket of snow." Bart was starting down the hall when he heard Tennyson call out for Carolyn again. He heard Sara quietly tell him, "I'm here, Tennyson. It will be alright, just relax and go back to sleep." Bart headed on down the stairs.

All night long and through the next day, Bart was in and out of the ranch house. He fetched bucket after bucket of snow and assisted Sara as she gave his boss the tonic. It wasn't until late in the afternoon that the fever broke and Tennyson started to cool down. His temperature was still up some, but he wasn't so burning hot. Sara left Bart with him long enough to go downstairs and fix some broth for him.

The next time Bart helped his boss sit up, Sara spooned some broth into him. This time he seemed to respond, and she was able to get some down him. He seemed to breathe easier when Bart laid him down on his pillow. Even Sara seemed to be hopeful he was over the worst of it.

Sara spoke, "Let's let him sleep now. Come downstairs with me and I'll fix us something to eat." She led the way and Bart followed.

As soon as they reached the kitchen, she poured him a cup of coffee that she had evidently made while she made the broth. In no time she had a skillet on the stove with bacon frying and was cutting slices of bread. Setting out the butter and jam, she went back to the skillet and turned the bacon. She set the table for two, put the bacon on a plate and broke several eggs into the iron skillet. Bart was surprised at the ease she had in the kitchen. She may be young, but not a beginner.

She set the plate of eggs on the table and sat down across from him. Before he could speak, she bowed her head and thanked God for Tennyson's improvement and prayed that he would continue to get well. She gave thanks for the help Bart had given and for the food before them.

When she finished, she surprised Bart once again as she picked up the eggs and dished some onto her plate, then bacon and bread. After spreading the butter and jam on her bread, she dug into the food on her plate before Bart had finished putting food on his plate. She looked up to see his surprised look.

"I haven't eaten since yesterday. I'm starved, and I'm not too shy or modest to admit it. That and the fact I've always had a good appetite. Tennyson says I eat like a field hand, but I don't cook like one." She smiled.

Bart smiled back. She could be a likeable person.

"Did you learn to cook because you came from a large family?" he asked, sure of the answer.

"No, I was an only child. I lost my mother when I was eight. I cooked and kept house for my father until he died when I was about thirteen. I was an indentured servant of sorts until I turned eighteen. I cooked and kept house for a family." Sara suddenly stopped talking. Why was she telling this to a stranger? She didn't know Bart. She better not say more than what was absolutely necessary.

"How long have you worked for Tennyson?" she asked, trying to turn the conversation away from herself.

"About twelve years. Tenn took on a greenhorn and took time to teach me how to run a ranch. How did you meet Tenn?" His curiosity was getting the better of his judgment.

Sara was gun shy now. "Eh, we met along the road north of Bloomfield. Would you like more eggs or bacon?"

"No, I'm fine."

"Well, if you would like, I'll fix up some bacon and bread for you in case you get hungry."

"That's not necessary. I'm going to have to go and check in with the hands. Do you need me to come back tonight?"

"I don't think that will be necessary. If I need you I'll put a light in the upstairs window facing the bunkhouse. And I'll shoot the gun to draw your attention. Will that work?"

"That should do it. Unless I get the signal, I'll check in with you in the morning as to how the Boss is doing."

"Yes, that will be fine." Sara walked over to him and put out her hand. "Thank you for your help today, Bart. I don't know what I would have done without it."

As he took her hand, Bart felt a warmth fill him. She withdrew her hand like she had been burnt. "I – I'd better go back upstairs and see how he is doing."

She was gone before Bart could speak. Somehow he found this strange girl causing a real contradiction of feelings in him. Who was she? Why was she here? What did she really want? Bart shook his head. Only the Lord could answer those questions. At least for now, he would try to take everything with a grain of salt. He looked down at his hand. He could still feel the warmth of her tiny hand in his. Slowly, Bart donned his coat, pulled on his boots and placing his hat atop his head, carried his gloves out into the cold. The storm had blown itself out sometime in the afternoon.

Now the world silently lay before him under a glistening white cover of snow. White in purity, it covered a multitude of sins. *Just like you do, Lord, with your blood. Thanks for the picture of your salvation. Lord, touch Boss and make him well. And Lord, lead me down the path You have for me. I'm thankin' You. Amen.*

CHAPTER THIRTY-SIX

RECOVERY

The next morning, another heavy snow was coming down again. When Bart returned to check on Tenn, he found him sitting up in bed playing checkers with Sara. Sara made the last jump on the board, winning the game.

"This game doesn't count, I'm a sick man," complained Tennyson.

"Oh yes, it counts. Don't try to fob off sickness on me. You worried me half to death with that fever, and until you *can* beat me in a game of checkers, you will stay in bed and every game you lose counts!" With that statement, Sara triumphantly picked up the checkers and board and set them on the side table. Then she started to leave the room. Meeting Bart at the door, she said, "Good morning! How's the snowstorm doing this morning?" She stopped long enough for an answer.

"Good morning, ma'am. Good morning, Boss. The storm is not quite as fierce, but the snow is still coming down. We have a good eight to ten inches in the pastures. If it keeps on snowing, we'll see a good foot to a foot and a half by evening."

"Are the men in the bunkhouse warm enough? Do they need anything?" asked Sara.

"No, ma'am. We're in good shape for now. We have plenty of supplies. Men just get a bit restless if they're cooped up more than three or four days."

Tennyson spoke up at this point and asked, "Do you think this storm is going to last that long?"

"I hope not, sir. I'm looking for it to blow itself out tonight. A sunny day could see quite a bit of snow melt, but flooding may be a problem. It's good we brought a good part of the herd in closer to home."

"I'll leave you two men to talk ranching. I've got some other things that need my attention. Excuse me." Sara slipped around Bart and out the door. As she passed, he was aware of a sweet smell of cinnamon and spice as she did so.

Bart walked over to the bed and sat down on the chair beside it.

"I understand I was out of my head with the fever," commented Tenn.

"That you were."

"I suppose I might have talked about Carolyn?" he asked.

"Not exactly. You thought Sara was Carolyn and kept calling her that. She seemed to handle it pretty well," replied Bart.

"Sara would never let on that anything I did bothered her. She knows I miss Carolyn. She herself said it was natural after all the years we were married to miss her. But I've got to make it up to Sara some way. Do you really think this storm will last long?"

"I don't think so. In another week, the roads should be open again. In a few days, one could travel if they have runners on their buggies or wagons."

"Then that's what I'll do. I want to take Sara to church come Sunday. That's four days away. Bart, I need you to get the buggy ready for a sleigh ride into town to attend church."

"Boss, are you going to feel up to doing that so soon? You were pretty sick last night."

"Certainly. I'll be up and around today. I just let Sara win a game now and then. That way she's willing to play me again. You get the sleigh ready, and I'll be up and around by the time we need it."

"Sure, Boss. Whatever you say. I'll get to it right away." Bart stood up and headed for the door. "I'll check back in with you later."

"See you then, Bart." Tennyson leaned back against his pillow and closed his eyes. Bart studied him for a moment and thought to himself that he didn't look all that well. He'd better talk with Sara about Boss's insistence on being up and about. Bart left the room intending to speak to Sara, and then go to the barn to see about putting runners on the buggy. At least that would give some of the men something to do.

Sara left the men upstairs and returned to the kitchen. She was in the process of making some soup for Tennyson when Bart returned on his way through to the back door. He stopped long enough to speak to Sara about Tenn.

"Did you know he plans on taking you to church this Sunday?" he asked her.

"Church? That Tennyson, he's always thinking of someone else. He knows it has been a good while since I've been able to go to church. I mentioned I would like to go sometime soon, but not this week-end in bad weather when he's still sick." She shook her head as she spoke the last few words.

"He wants me to put runners on the buggy so you can go this weekend. I'll do it, because that's what he wants, but I thought you should know. He still looks a little peaked to me."

"I know. I think he is trying to convince himself he is not sick, but I know differently. I guess we'll just have to take it one day at a time. I do wish the doctor could come out to see him and check him over."

"Maybe if the weather cooperates, I could go in with the sleigh and bring the doctor out, but how will we convince Boss that he needs to be seen by the doctor?" Bart rubbed his forehead.

"I know how to convince him," replied Sara. "I'll tell him that I need the doctor. He'll buy that. How soon do you think you could go in to fetch him?"

"The day after tomorrow would probably be the earliest. I'll plan on doing it then. You make sure Tenn isn't suspicious."

"I'll do my best. And Bart," Bart paused at the door, "thanks for helping me tend to Tennyson. You were a big help to me in taking care of him. I don't know what I would have done without you."

"Sure. Glad I could help." He tipped his hat and left.

Sara watched him cross over the yard in the deep snow and make his way back to the barn. Bart was someone she knew she could count on . . . *now what did that mean?* Sara muttered to herself as she turned back to her soup.

When she fed Tennyson the soup, she mentioned she sure would like to have a doctor check her over and make sure everything was alright with the baby. He looked at her a long time before replying.

"I suppose while the doctor is here, he might as well check me over, too. Will that make you feel better, Sara?"

"How did you know? Tennyson, you're incorrigible. Yes, I think the doctor should see you. Your color isn't good, and I don't want anything to happen to you. I'd feel lost without you."

"Okay, bring the doctor here and he can check both of us out. But if he gives us both a clean bill of health, then you be ready for church on Sunday. Agreed?"

"Agreed!"

"Good! That settles that. Now, if you don't mind, I need to get my beauty sleep before the doctor comes. I want to have roses in my cheeks when he checks me."

"You're more apt to be black and blue from the skillet I'll use if you don't behave!" said Sarah with a grin as she left the room and quietly closed the door. *Thank you, Lord, that he didn't resist having the doctor check him over. Watch over my husband, Lord.*

CHAPTER THIRTY-SEVEN
CHURCH

The storm did not abate that night. The temperature had dropped well below freezing. The wind picked up and snow swirled around in gales, blowing and drifting, causing travel of any kind to be hazardous. Ropes were tied from the bunkhouse to the cook shack, to the barn and even to the house, so men wouldn't lose their way in the storm. Ice encrusted the ground and even made walking hazardous.

Bart tried to make his way up to the house in the morning and evening, but Sara and Tennyson were both fine. Tennyson was up and around and his color had returned to his face. Sara told Bart not to worry about the doctor as it didn't look like it was necessary.

It was Sunday before the storm had truly blown itself out and the sun reappeared in the sky. The world was a white wonderland reflecting the brightness of the sun. The men started digging themselves out with paths that led here and there, following the lead of the ropes. They had had their hands full in caring for the calves and cows in the barn area. They put runners on the hay wagon in order to get hay to the other parts of the range for the cattle there. The storm had been bad and they were holding their breaths to see how much damage it had actually done.

By Wednesday, the damage was known. A third of the herd left on the range had frozen in the storm. Only a couple of head was lost in the herd that had been brought in closer to the barn. The final tally showed about a fourth of the herd overall had been lost, not counting the calves. The calves brought the total herd back up to where it had been the year before. There would not be a large herd to drive to market, but they also wouldn't be taking a loss.

The melting snow was causing flooding in the low areas. It made travel difficult and the men had to watch for cattle getting bogged down in the mud. By Friday, Tennyson was on a horse and going over the range with Bart to see the damage and how things were progressing. Although the loss would hurt their profit for the year, it would not put them in the red, and Tennyson knew they had been more fortunate than other ranches that had lost over half of their herds. Again, Tenn thanked Bart for his foresight in bringing a good part of the cows and calves in closer where they could help protect them. His actions had made the difference.

CHURCH

Tennyson arrived back at the house and told Sara to pack her bags for they would leave Saturday morning for town. They could get needed supplies, check in with the doctor, stay the night at the hotel and go to church the next day before coming home. "It will give us both a chance to get out of the house. Now don't forget to pack that pretty rosebud dress and hat I like so well."

Sara beamed at the chance to get away for a day or two as she had grown a little weary of being inside. *Now why was that?* She thought about it. *I was inside the cabin for longer periods than this and it didn't bother me. Something inside of me is restless for what, I don't know.*

The next morning, Tennyson and Sara drove off in the buggy for their outing. Bart saw them off as he had brought the buggy around to the front door. As he watched them leave, his heart felt heavy. He shook his head. There was no reason for him to have a heavy heart, he had work to do for the Boss and that's what mattered. If he got everything done, maybe he could make church tomorrow. It had been a while since he had been there. Bart left for the barn whistling a tune.

Sara and Tennyson had a grand time in town. They were both checked by the doctor and declared fit, although the doctor had warned both of them to take it easy. Sara was starting her fifth month and was growing around the middle. Tennyson's age was to be taken into consideration as he was not a young man any longer. Both said they would, but neither saw it as necessary for themselves, just for the other one.

    Tennyson left Sara to do some shopping while he ordered supplies to be picked up on Monday by one of his men. He also visited the lawyer's office and the Judge making sure things were to his satisfaction. He stopped at the telegraph office and sent two telegrams to inform his children of his recent marriage. *That should stir things up with both of them. I wouldn't be surprised if they don't come to visit during the next few weeks.* He grinned to himself at the looks on their faces when they read the news. Then he sobered a little. *I'd better warn Sara about it. But I'll wait 'til we're back home. I don't want to spoil the trip for her.*

    The next morning, Sara dressed in her rosebud dress, noticing it was already getting snug around the middle. She would have to forgo wearing it for a few months. Tennyson put on his suit and Sara told him they were both so pretty, that they would be the talk of Bloomfield.

    "Sara, we're already the talk of the town, and not because of what we're wearing," chuckled Tennyson.

    "Wait until I really start showing. Then *you'll* be the talk of the town," she answered saucily.

    "Well, you might have a point. Talk is what people are good at. I hope you don't mind being the subject of their conversations."

"Tennyson, I don't mind. I've not forgotten all that you have done for me. I am thankful to be your wife, and I will be the best wife I know how to be for the best hero of a husband any woman could have."

"Now there you've gone and made me blush. Sara, I know you're young and I know your heart is in the right place. I just don't want any gossip to hurt you or our child."

"It won't. Not as long as I have you to be there for me. I can get through it."

"Well, that's the easy part. Now, Mrs. Keye, if you're ready, let's go to church."

"Lead the way, Mr. Keye. I'll follow."

The Keyes made a sensation at church. Many people had heard about the marriage and what had happened in town, but they had not seen them together for themselves. Many suspected the young lady was a gold-digger, but they met them with smiles and congratulations just the same.

The service was simple and the sermon's text was based on Luke 11:1-10. In the passage, the disciples asked Jesus to teach them how to pray. The pastor said that people failed to find power in prayer because they failed to understand how prayer works.

"First, we must acknowledge God. 'Our Father' alone requires that the one praying must have a relationship with God before they can call him Father. You must be a part of the family of God. The only way you can do this is by asking Jesus Christ to come into your heart, apply the blood He shed at Calvary to wash away your sin, and become your Lord and Savior. If you haven't done that at some point in your life, then the only prayer God will hear from you is the one begging for salvation. All other prayers will fall on deaf ears, for God is not your Father.

"'Our Father, who art in heaven, Hallowed be thy name.' We cannot forget who we are praying to, God Almighty, who resides in heaven and is the Creator of the universe. 'Thy kingdom come. Thy will be done, as in heaven, so in earth.' We must understand that through Jesus Christ, we have access to God the Father. Do you have access? Have you asked the Savior to forgive you of your sins? Remember He is coming one day to establish His kingdom and every knee shall bow and every tongue confess that He is Lord, Savior, and King.

"'Give us day by day our daily bread.' We are not told to ask for it a week or a month at a time, but daily. We must seek Him each and every day for His provision to meet the needs that we have. It is like the manna that came from heaven to the Israelites as they journeyed through the wilderness. Each and every day they were told to go and gather for that day. It did not last longer than one day, and no one gathered too little or too much. God provided what was needed for the day. Only on the day before the Sabbath did the manna last for more than a day. God wants us to seek Him each and every day for the needs that we have for that day. We are not to worry about next week's or next month's, we ask only for today.

"'And forgive us our sins; for we also forgive everyone that is indebted to us.' That is a mighty big statement right there. Have you forgiven everyone that is indebted to you, that has hurt you, tormented you, owes you, angered you or cheated you out of something dear to you? How can we ask God to forgive us if we can't forgive another? How can we ask Him for something we aren't willing to give to others? I don't know about you, but that hits me pretty close to home. I fail so often. That's why we need to come to Him daily and seek forgiveness.

"I would add one more passage to what we have read today. In John 14, verses 13 and 14, Jesus gives a new privilege we can have in prayer. 'And whatever ye shall ask in my name, that will I do, that the Father may be glorified in the Son. If ye shall ask anything in my name, I will do it.' What a promise to the children of God! Do you need to come forward today and ask something of God in the name of Jesus?"

As the pastor, continued drawing his message to a close, Sara sat stunned in her seat. She had never forgiven Jud for what he had taken from her, her innocence. She had never forgiven Jud for pursuing her and hunting her down. She had failed to forgive him in her heart and it would always haunt her, unless she could do it. She looked at Tennyson with tears in her eyes.

"Tennyson, I need to forgive Jud for what he did to me or else he wins and I lose."

"Sara, that is between you and the Lord. Do you want me to go with you?"

"No, I can do it if it's alright with you. I am just a bit scared, though."

"It is fine with me. I probably need to do some forgiving in that department myself. Let's go up together, but we can pray individually."

Quietly, during the altar call, Tennyson stepped out and allowing Sara to go before, walked up to the altar with her as they both knelt and prayed. When he had finished, he simply stood, waited for her and helped her stand when she finished, then they walked back to their seats together.

In the back of the church sat Bart. He watched as Sara went forward and prayed. There must have been something on her mind to cause her to weep so. He also watched how Tennyson tenderly waited for her and how thankful she was to him. There was some secret behind their marriage. Bart had to admit that Sara was not looking for money in this marriage. What was she looking for and why did it bother Bart so? *Lord, help me understand or else change my thinking as I sure seem to be interested in Sara and why she is married to Tenn.*

As the final benediction was being given, Bart slipped out the door, stepped up into the saddle of his horse, and turned it in the direction of the ranch. He had a lot of thinking to do.

CHAPTER THIRTY-EIGHT

ANTICIPATION

On the drive home from church, Tennyson told Sara he needed to talk to her about something that might come up.

"Sara, you know I have grown children and grandchildren."

"Yes, I remember you telling me about them."

"Well, I have reason to believe we might be getting a visit from them in the next couple of weeks and I wanted to warn you about it, so you can kind of prepare yourself for the event."

"I see. And just what makes you suspect that they might be coming?"

"Well, the telegrams I sent."

"I see. And when did you send these telegrams, may I ask?"

"Certainly, certainly, you can ask me anything!" answered Tennyson.

"When?"

"When what?"

Sara sighed. "Tennyson, I think you'd better turn this buggy around and head back into town."

"Whatever for?" he asked in surprise.

"Because I feel a need to go back to the altar again and do some more forgiving! Now, when did you send the telegrams?"

"Yesterday. I thought it was only right that I tell my own flesh and blood that I had married again."

"That's better. I agree, you needed to tell them, although if I were your child, I would be a little upset finding out about it five months after the marriage," commented Sara.

"Would you now? It's lucky for me you're my wife and not my daughter, I'm thinking."

"I see. It's nice to know you're thinking." Sara was silent for a moment. "While you're thinking, what do you think will happen when your daughter and son meet me for the first time?"

Tennyson ducked his head and shook it a little.

"I'm not sure I want to think about that."

"Oh, give it a try just for the fun of it."

"Well, have you ever seen fireworks at a Fourth of July Celebration?"

"I've seen them."

"You might want to increase it, even double it, in comparison with the fireworks I'm kind of expecting."

"Hmmm. And as your wife, you expect me to be ready for this conflagration?"

"Well, I was hoping you might be up for it."

"Really. I think, Tennyson Keye, I'll just head back to the mountain cabin for the next

ANTICIPATION

three months until the baby is due. Or you can come and get me after the fireworks are over." Sara seemed satisfied with her plan.

"Sara, would you really leave me here alone to face them?" He grinned. "You know they are by right, your step-children, and I think as their stepmother you ought to be here." He looked as pitiful as he could.

Sara gave him a long sideways stare. Then she looked straight ahead and with a deadpan face replied, "One word in the presence of your children of my being their stepmother, and you, Tennyson Keye, will find yourself explaining to your men why you have to move into the bunkhouse with them. Understood?"

"Yes ma'am," he answered meekly, "understood."

"Very well, I won't go to the cabin. But Tennyson, I want you to make your offspring understand that I do not want to cause them any problems as far as seeing their father or inheriting the ranch from him. You married me to save me when I needed saving, and I'm here today because you are a man of honor and compassion. I will not tolerate them accusing you of anything less."

"Thank you, Sara. I knew I could depend on you. Josie and Ned are bound to be upset, especially when they see how young you are. But I want you to know, I don't plan to tell them the details of why we are married. They will have to either trust me that I was not senile, or drunk at the time, or just learn to live with it."

"Tennyson, what will they say when they learn of the baby I'm carrying?"

"Well, there you have me. I have no clue. I thought I might keep that a secret a little while longer," he looked down at her middle, even though she had a cloak on, "but I guess I'm not going to be able to do that much longer."

"I don't think so either. You've got to realize that you are shaking their entire world up and that won't set easy with them."

"You're right, Sara. It looks like we're going to have to spend some time on our knees and give this to the Lord. I'm starting to understand what Abraham went through more and more these days. He was a hundred years old when he had his son. I can sympathize with him. I'm even starting to think the name of the baby should be Isaac."

"Isaac. I like that. Isaac T Keye." Sara smiled to herself, and then asked, "What if it's a girl?"

"That I haven't thought about," he remarked.

"Do you have a favorite name?"

Tennyson was silent a moment, then said, "Arabella Lacy."

"Arabella Lacy," repeated Sara, "that's an unusual name. Did you know someone by that name?"

"It was my mother's name, Arabella Lacy. I always thought it was beautiful."

"Arabella Lacy Keye, it is. I think it is beautiful, too. It flows like a piece of music."

By that time, they had reached the turn and the ranch lay before them. Although the snow was still in piles everywhere, the ranch was a wondrous thing to see. Sara spoke softly to Tennyson.

"It *is* so beautiful, but I still think the mountain cabin is even more so." She smiled up into his eyes.

"That's because *you* were there to make it so. Now you make the ranch beautiful. Thank you, wife, for being you." With that he flipped the reins and the buggy moved on down the road towards the ranch.

CHAPTER THIRTY-NINE
OFFSPRING

*B*oth of the Keyes were surprised when a month came and went and neither of Tennyson's children came or made contact. He said he didn't know what to make of it, but he was still certain they would show up sooner or later. Sara didn't know and wasn't taking any chances. She prayed daily for Josie and Ned and meeting them for the first time. She asked the Lord to guide her, direct her tongue in the things she would say to them, and that they would not be upset with their father for marrying again.

During those weeks, Sara found herself growing to the point she wore old skirts and lose tops that were serviceable, but not very attractive. Tennyson took her into town one day and she went to the dressmaker and ordered two skirts with full blouses and one nice dress for Sundays.

She had them picked up the following week when Bart went in for supplies. She told Tennyson that she felt guilty for spending money on clothes, but she also didn't want to embarrass him in front of his children.

"If you and I were still back at the cabin, it wouldn't matter and I could make do with what I have. This way, I'm spending your money on clothes that will only be good for a few months, and just because of vanity over how I look," she complained, "but I do want to look the best I can for your sake."

Tennyson grinned. "I'm sorry, but you'll just have to bite the bullet. I can handle the cost of the clothes. I'll just take it out of your wages."

"What? You don't supply uniforms for the help? I'm going to have to look elsewhere for employment. I do all this work and no benefits!" She grinned at him.

"No benefits at all? Are you sure?" He said with a lifted eyebrow.

"I can't think of any." She said with an innocent look.

"What about the bed warmer you take advantage of every night?"

She giggled. "I do use him as a foot warmer, don't I."

"Don't I know it!"

"Well, I guess there are a few benefits. I can think of another."

"You can? Would you care to share?"

"That's it; I care to share – to share life with my hero. Tennyson, you are a blessing to me from God. One I thank Him for every day."

Tennyson hugged her and kissed her on top of her forehead. "You can buy a new dress anytime."

Two weeks later, Sara was out working in the garden in one of her old skirts and top. Tennyson had left a couple of hours before to go check on some of the cattle with Bart. She was doing some weeding when she heard and saw a buggy coming. She could make out a man and woman. Suddenly, she remembered how she was dressed – in the oldest clothes she had! As quickly as she was able, Sara got to her feet and hurried to the back door and up to the bedroom. She changed into one of the new skirts and tops. She brushed her hair back and put a clasp around it. She actually heard someone downstairs in the living room. It must be Tennyson's offspring for them to come into the house without knocking.

As she came down the stairs, she heard loud voices coming from the living room.

"Maybe he's just gone senile!" remarked a female voice.

"Not Dad. He probably picked her up at a saloon and was too drunk to know what he was doing," answered a male voice.

"That's ridiculous! Dad doesn't drink or go into saloons and well you know it. I just can't understand him marrying a younger woman. I wonder how young. It would be terrible if she and I were the same age."

"We're not," interrupted Sara as she entered the room, "I believe I'm several years younger than you."

"You must be a gold-digger to marry someone as old as Dad. He is old enough . . ." but Sara cut the man off in the middle of his sentence.

"He's old enough to know what he is doing and doesn't make snap decisions. He didn't marry me within a week of meeting me. He thought long and hard about it. I didn't marry him for his money. When I met and knew Tennyson, I didn't know he even had any money. I did know he had a ranch, but that meant nothing to me, because he also told me he had two children who would inherit, and I told him from the beginning that I will not have anything that belongs to his children taken from them."

"He married you because you are pregnant. Giving your child a name is what he did. It sounds like something Dad would do." said Ned.

If you knew the truth, you would know how close you are to it. Sara looked at him steadily and answered, "Mr. Keye, if you would like to see our marriage certificate, you would find we were married six weeks before I conceived with this child. Your father had his reasons, but it is up to him to tell you and not me. I can only tell you that I owe your father a great deal. I have no plans to replace your mother in your lives, thank goodness, or in his. But I will be the best wife that I can be for such an honorable and decent man."

There was silence in the room. Both Josie and Ned looked at each other.

Finally, Sara said, "Excuse me, I must see about dinner." Sara silently left the room and headed for the kitchen. *Lord, let my words be received in the manner they were intended. Don't let them be angry at their father, but help them to understand how lonely life can be. Guide me, Father, and help me to be the best wife I can be. I know that will only be possible if You make it so. Amen.*

Tennyson was in one of the outlying areas of the ranch with Bart checking on cattle when he got word there were visitors at the house. Tennyson told Bart he had to get back there as soon as he could.

"They could eat Sara alive and spit her out before I can get there. I knew better than to come this far away. Bart, let's head back. I may need you to keep me from murdering my own children if they've hurt Sara in any way."

"Yes, Boss. I'm right behind you."

Both riders turned their mounts and galloped in the direction of the ranch house. Tennyson thought they would never get there. Bart feared for Sara as well. As much as he would have liked to ride past the boss and go ahead, Bart stayed back behind him and let him set the pace. Both riders had stern looks as they rode their horses hard across the rolling hills.

Sara had checked the stew she had had cooking since late that morning. She needed some kind of dessert to go with the stew and dumplings. As she looked through the larder, she decided on some peach cobbler. She could bake that and it wasn't hard to put together. She was busy working with the ingredients for the cobbler when she heard a voice being cleared. She turned to find both of Tennyson's children standing before her with something to say.

"I'm not sure how to address you," fumbled Ned.

"Just call me Sara."

"Well, Sara, we want to apologize to you for the things we said. We were both shocked and surprised to learn Dad had married six months ago and never said a word to us. I guess it made me angry that he did so. I just couldn't understand why he would want to marry anyone else, besides Mom."

"I can understand your feelings, Mr. Keye."

"Ned, please, and this is Josie."

"Alright, Ned, Josie, your apology is accepted. It's understandable since you've both lost your mother and it hasn't been that long. I know what it is like to lose your parent. That's why I said I can't and won't even try to replace your mother to you or your Dad. I can't. I can only be me, Sara, and do the best that I can do."

Josie spoke up, "It's a little hard for us to think he married someone younger than we are."

Sara chuckled, "Don't I know it. I threatened to banish Tennyson to the bunkhouse if he ever used the term stepmother around me."

Josie shook her head, "It's hard to imagine you threatening Dad." She nodded to Sara's midriff, or lack thereof, and said, "It's also hard to imagine that at my age I'm going to have a new half brother or sister."

Sara slowly nodded, "It's been hard for your father to imagine having to deal with diapers again on someone who is not a grandchild. As for me, I just take each day as the Lord gives. Now, if you don't mind, I need to get this cobbler finished up and in the oven if we're going to have it for dinner tonight."

"Here, let me help you," volunteered Josie.

"While you girls do that, I'll carry in the luggage. What rooms do you want us in, Sara?" asked Ned before leaving the kitchen.

"Your own rooms are ready for you. Make yourself at home, because that's what this still is, only slightly different. I'm not very tall, you can overlook me." Sara laughed, "That is, if you can get around me."

Josie asked, "How far along are you?"

Sara replied, "I am in my sixth month. I think I look like I'm in my last month."

"I thought I was going to have triplets, but I only had one." Josie smiled. "They are a wonder from God, though."

Sara smiled, "That they are."

Unexpectedly, they both heard a ruckus in the living room. Tennyson's voice could be heard shouting at Ned. Sara and Josie both rushed into the room to find Ned, Tennyson and Bart staring at each other with angry faces.

Ned was emphatically speaking, "You have no right to yell at me when you waited six months before telling us you were married. Dad, come on. I'm angry, yes, but not at Sara. I'm mad at *you* for not trusting us with the truth about your marriage."

Tennyson stopped for a second before asking, "You're not mad at Sara?"

Ned looked towards the doorway where Josie and Sara had just come in to the room. Sara was so much smaller than Josie, at least in height, that he turned back to his dad and said, "Who could be mad at Sara? There's not even enough there to be mad at if you wanted to be."

"You mean, you're alright with Sara being my wife? And the mother of my child?" spoke Tennyson in wonder.

"As your wife, yes. As for being the mother of *your* child, that will take a little getting used to for me," admitted Ned.

"And you, too, Josie?" asked her Dad.

"Me, too. Although we did say a few things at first, which Sara set us straight on, and we have apologized for them. I guess we can deal with the situation." Josie smiled at Sara.

"Well, Tennyson. You certainly have a way of greeting guests. Supper will be ready in about half an hour. Until then," Sara went to a chair and sat down, "I'm off my feet. Josie, everything is ready if you don't mind serving. My feet are killing me."

"Ah, excuse me, Boss. I'd better tend to our horses. I'll give them a good rub down and feed them. It was nice seeing you again, Ned, Josie." Bart ducked back out the front door and took the horses out to the barn.

Later that night, after everyone had gone to bed, Tennyson looked at Sara.

"You know I busted my tail getting back here when I heard Ned and Josie were here. I thought maybe they had eaten you alive."

Sara smiled, "I know. That's because you're my hero; always coming to my rescue."

"I just can't believe it. I was certain that they would give you a hard time and I would find you devastated and in tears."

"Well, it just goes to show you what the power of prayer can do," said Sara sleepily. She yawned. "I've been praying about this day ever since you told me about the telegrams."

"Ned said you set them straight. I sure wish I could have been here to have seen that. Tell me, Sara, what did you say to them?"

Tennyson didn't get an answer, so he turned to look at Sara. She was fast asleep. He lay back on his pillow and looked up. *Well, Lord, once again You have shown me that You are in charge and not me. Thanks for taking care of Sara today. She is special. Bless her and the child she's carrying. Bless the time we have together with Ned and Josie and I'll be thanking You for Your watch care. Amen.*

CHAPTER FORTY

CONFESSIONS

Josie and Ned stayed for one more day before leaving for town to catch the train back to their homes. During that day, Ned rode with his father over the ranch and they talked about the details of it and how the ranch had escaped severe loss by moving part of the herd closer to the barn when they did.

Ned told his father that his ranch was doing well, but it was nothing like his dad's place. This surprised Tennyson and they talked about what Ned would like to do. Ned told his dad that he would like to return to Bloomfield and have the ranch someday. Tennyson told him not to give up on his dream or do anything foolish for another year. Ned looked at his dad.

"Dad, what is that supposed to mean?" asked a puzzled Ned.

"Oh, I just feel a stirring in the wind, so to speak. I think if you just bide your time, you'll be satisfied in the long run." replied Tennyson. He held out his hand. "Agreed?"

Ned shook his head a little, but grasped his father's hand and answered, "Agreed."

Josie and Sara got along fine. Sara was open to Josie's suggestions and advice, which made Josie feel very comfortable around this "step-mother" who was absolutely no threat to her. Josie had done some thinking and asked Sara if she minded her asking some personal questions.

"Personal, you say?" Sara hesitated. "Well, I guess not. If they are, I won't answer, but promise you won't get mad at me if I don't."

"I promise." Josie smiled. "Sara, since Dad isn't a spring chicken, what do you plan to do when he is gone? Have you made any plans for that?"

Sara got real quiet. "Honestly, Josie, I haven't. But I won't be any worse off than I was before. Better, in fact, thanks to your Dad. I don't have any family. The tough part would be finding me a job somewhere, but I'll trust my heavenly Father to provide for me as He always does."

"The reason I asked is I would like for you to come and stay with me a while until you get your bearings. Jeff and I, as well as our son, Andrew, would love to have you. You could help me with the house and the new baby."

Sara looked at Josie quickly and asked, "Josie, are you having another baby?"

"Yes, my husband and I are so excited. We hope this one will be a girl." Josie beamed.

"Your dad will be so happy and so proud," exclaimed Sara.

"So happy and proud about what?" asked Tennyson as he and Ned entered the room.

"Josie, tell him," urged Sara.

"Jeff and I are going to have another baby come harvest time," spoke Josie.

"A baby, that's wonderful!" shouted Tennyson as he went over and hugged Josie.

"Eh, Dad, I almost forgot to tell you," interrupted Ned, "that Maryann and I are expecting, too."

"You and Maryann? When is it due?" asked Tennyson in amazement.

"About two months. That's why she didn't make the trip here. But we're excited about the news."

"Boy, are you two ever the quiet ones. Been here almost twenty-four hours and not tell me I'm going to be a Grandpa again. And you claimed I was the close-mouthed one."

Ned chuckled. "You have to admit, Dad, your news was a lot more to handle than a simple announcement of the birth of a baby – and you had that announcement, too."

Sara decided it was time to look at the lighter side of the situation and added, "So if I have this right, both of you will have babies close to the time their uncle is born or shortly after?"

Everyone stopped and looked at Sara.

"I never thought of that," remarked Tennyson. "Our baby will be their uncle, or aunt as the case may be, and their grandma will be younger than either of their . . ."

"Tennyson! The bunkhouse could still be your future!" interrupted Sara.

"Yes, ma'am," was all Tennyson would say.

Josie and Ned looked at each other and began laughing. Soon, everyone was laughing, then all started in again with questions and comments about the upcoming events when Sara slipped out to fix some lunch.

After his children had both left, Tennyson remarked to Sara, "I think that has been the best visit I ever had with my children. Before Carolyn died, I was too busy to bother much with them while they were here. After she died, it was strained, and then they just didn't come."

"I'm glad that it wasn't that way this time, and you enjoyed them. It is amazing how well everything went. We have the Lord to thank for that." Sara yawned. "I think I'm ready to go to bed. This baby wears me out quicker than baling hay."

"Baling hay? When did you ever bale hay?" asked Tennyson.

"I didn't. But getting enough food ready to feed the crew that did, just about wore me out, and that didn't count all the cleaning up that had to be done afterward."

"Well, then, Mrs. Keye, let me escort you to your bed."

"Do you have designs on me?" she whispered with a look of desperation.

"No, I don't have designs on you," whispered Tennyson back to her. "It's just I've been riding all day and these old bones are about jarred out of place. Laying on a bed sounds mighty appealing."

"Lead on, then, sir. I'll follow your every step." giggled Sara.

"Married women don't giggle, Sara," admonished Tennyson.

"This married woman does," Sara stated, then giggled again.

CHAPTER FORTY-ONE
FIREWORKS

The Fourth of July was fast approaching. Tennyson had been asked to deliver a speech just before the fireworks about the history of Bloomfield, as he had been one of the first men to settle in the area. Tennyson was honored to be asked and had spent many an evening working on his speech.

The whole day promised to be exciting. There were to be all types of games and contests during the afternoon as well as a race through town. Bart and several of the ranch hands were entering that. Late in the afternoon, would be the potluck dinner followed by a dance until dusk. Then would come the speeches and the grand finale would be the fireworks.

Everyone was looking forward to the day. Sara felt like she had grown twice as large as the month before and could hardly believe she still had August and September to get through. She felt pretty good except for her feet if she was on them long. They would swell up easily if she didn't take time to lie down and rest. She didn't say anything to Tennyson about them, as he had enough on his plate with his speech, without worrying about her.

Finally, the day arrived bright and clear. No clouds to threaten rain, just a bright sun promising a warm day to enjoy outside.

Tennyson had brought the buggy around and helped Sara in, after stowing away all the food she had prepared for the day. They enjoyed the ride into town, arriving to crowds of bustling people, who were strolling the streets and greeting one another.

Tennyson had arranged with the livery to stow his horse and carriage, so he knew he didn't need to park outside of town, and have to walk a ways to get back into town. He and Sara walked the streets and stopped for lunch at a crowded cafe, finding a table for the two of them. Tennyson even stopped in at the hotel to see if he could get a room, but they were completely booked up with guests.

"I should have thought of it sooner," Tennyson remonstrated with himself. "You really should lie down and rest."

"Tennyson, I'm doing fine. Let's not worry about it and enjoy the day."

Afterward, they watched the games and the antics of the young people as they competed in games of penny scramble, pie-eating, and three-legged races. The older teens competed in races, too, as well as an egg tossing contest which concluded with some messy results.

The last event of the afternoon was the horse race. There were about a dozen men in a heat and there were three heats before the final race. Bart was the only one of the ranch hands that made it to the final race. Tennyson and Sara cheered him on as the gun sounded and the riders left the starting point in front of the bank. They actually raced out of town for half a mile at a designated turning place in the road, then back through town for the finish. There were men stationed to make sure all competitors made it to the turn.

As the riders rode out of sight, the crowd in town waited in anticipation of the return of the racers. Sara was so proud at how well Bart had done in the primary races and she hoped he would win overall. He was such a good rider and fast. Tennyson said that Bart was one of the favorites to win.

Suddenly, a shout went up and everyone looked down the street waiting for the appearance of the returning riders. Sure enough, Bart was one of the leaders as they thundered into sight. Bart called something to his horse, and Sampson started to pick up speed. By the time they reached the finished line, Bart was ahead of everyone else and won first place. Bart slowed his horse down, and then walked Sampson back to the finish line. Everyone cheered as he was awarded his ribbon.

As he came by Tennyson and Sara, he stopped as they congratulated him, then he slowly walked Sampson back to the livery to rub him down, water and feed him for a job well done.

Once the race was over, the crowd flocked to the tables for the potluck dinner. The pastor of the church quieted everyone down. He thanked the Lord for the town, for His blessings on the people who lived in Bloomfield, and for His bounty. Then with his hearty "Amen," everyone broke out in a cheer and got in line to enjoy some of the bounty.

Sara saved a place for Tennyson as he stood in line and filled two plates for them. Bart surprised her by placing two glasses of iced tea down for her and the boss before joining the line with the rest. She and Tennyson enjoyed the meal. Try as she might, Sara didn't see Bart again, except when she spotted him with some of the other cowhands who were eating by a corral.

Following the potluck was the dance. By the time Sara and Tennyson had loaded all of her dishes into the buggy, Sara knew her feet had swollen. She didn't dare look for fear Tennyson would see, and she didn't want to spoil his day. When they returned, the dance was well underway, and she and Tennyson found seats off to one side and sat watching the dancers. Finally, a waltz began to play. Tennyson stood and offered his hand to Sara. She took his hand and tugged on it.

"Offering me your hand, fine sir, is so kind. But if you don't use that hand to help me get up, it will be all for nothing," she said prettily.

Tennyson laughed and offered both hands and got her to her feet. She stepped into his arms and they joined the swirling couples. About twice around the floor and there was a commotion at the doorway. A couple of men motioned to Tennyson to join them. Tennyson looked around and spied Bart, nodding for him to come over to them.

"I've been called outside by the committee. They probably want to finalize the ceremony before the fireworks. Will you finish this dance with Sara? It's the only one she has had, and I don't want to disappoint her by stopping it."

"Sure, Boss." And the exchange was made.

"May I?" asked Bart to Sara and held out his hand.

"Thank you," replied Sara. As she placed her hand into Bart's and felt his arm go around her, she felt a warmth she had never experienced before. Bart was taller than Tennyson and she only came up to his chest. As she peeked up into his face, she found his smiling eyes looking into hers. For a moment, she was lost in the depths of their blueness as she moved around and around the floor in his arms.

Someone bumped into Bart, and the sudden jerk shook Sara out of her trance. She was dancing with someone not her husband, and she was having the strangest feelings. She didn't dare look up again into Bart's face, but her mind raced as she faced the feelings she was having. She was in love with Bart! She now realized why she trusted him and went to him when she needed help. It was a good thing that her pregnancy kept them at arm's length on the dance floor or she would be in trouble!

The realization shook Sara to her very being and she slightly stumbled a step in the dance.

"Are you all right, Sara?" Bart's low voice crowded into her thoughts.

"Yes, but I'm feeling tired. Could we sit the rest of this dance out? I think I should get off of my feet."

He escorted her to her chair and left her to get them some punch. Sara needed the time to compose herself. It made no difference how she felt about Bart, she was the wife of Tennyson, her hero, and she would never do anything to jeopardize that. Sara's head started to ache. She knew she was tired and her feet were hurting. She peeked at one by lifting the edge of her skirt and sure enough, her ankles had completely disappeared. What she wouldn't give to slip into her moccasins and put her feet up.

Tennyson reappeared about the same time Bart returned with the punch. They both took one look at Sara and voiced their concerns.

"I'm all right," insisted Sara. "It's just been a long day and I'm exhausted."

"I'll take you home," stated Tennyson.

"No, you have to make your speech. You've worked on it so hard, Tennyson, and I want you to make it." Sara was adamant.

"Well, if you insist. But I think you should still go home. I saw your feet, Sara. Why didn't you tell me sooner? Bart, would you drive Sara home in the buggy and see she is settled in, then you can return. You should have enough time before the fireworks start."

"I'd be glad to, Boss," was Bart's reply.

"No, I'll stay here. I don't want to miss your speech, Tennyson," said Sara.

"Bart, go get the buggy." Bart left to do his boss's bidding. "Sara, you've heard my speech over and over. You and the baby need to go home and rest. I insist. I am ashamed of myself that I didn't take you home sooner, before the dance."

"But Tennyson, you promised to dance with me."

"And I did, or at least tried to before we were interrupted. I think I hear the buggy. Come along, Sara. You're going home." Tennyson helped her to her feet and walked out to the buggy with her, helping her into the back seat."

"Bart, take it easy with her and try not to jar her." He turned to Sara. He kissed her hand and said, "I'll see you at home and tell you all about the speech and the fireworks."

"Promise you'll wake me up if I fall asleep?"

"I promise, Sara. Off with you now. Bart, I'll see you later."

Bart pulled away and started the buggy down the street and out of town. He drove in silence for three or four miles. He thought Sara may have dozed off in the back.

Well, Bart thought to himself, *you know for sure now – one brief, but glorious dance with*

Sara in your arms, and you knew you had fallen for her completely. You love her and have loved her since you first laid eyes on her; a woman who is already married and carrying another man's child.

Lord, prayed Bart, *what is wrong with me? Why should I feel so strongly about her? Is this part of Your plan for me; to love a married woman? Is this a test to see if I am an honorable man? I don't know if I can pass that test, not with these feelings. Guide me, Lord; keep me from doing what will displease you.*

Bart wondered if it was Satan tempting him. It made no difference. It didn't change anything. Now he knew why he made excuses to go to the house to check with the boss over incidental matters. He went hoping to get a glimpse of Sara or a chance to speak with her. Now that he knew for certain how he felt, it would be harder than ever to keep his distance. Bart groaned.

"Bart, are you alright?' questioned Sara.

"Sara," Bart came to himself, "I'm fine. Just reacting to a thought and didn't realize I did it out loud."

"You felt it, too, didn't you, Bart – when we danced?" said Sara timidly.

Bart stopped the horse on the solitary road and turned to look back at the little lady that had stolen his heart.

"Sara, I have to admit that tonight I realized something I should have known long before now. You see, Sara, I'm in . . ."

"Don't say it, Bart," Sara urgently pleaded. "We can't say it. We have no right to say it, even if it is true. Bart, I'm married to the man who has saved my life time and time again. He's my hero and a most honorable man. You know yourself what he did for you, taking you on and teaching you about ranching. I cannot – I will not do anything that would hurt him or dishonor his good name in any fashion. I took a sacred vow before God and I will honor that vow even if it costs me the greatest happiness in the world. So you best turn back around and head this buggy for the Keye Ranch, for that's where I'm staying until the good Lord Himself closes our vows through death, which I pray won't come for a long time." Sara was overwrought now.

"Is that what you want, Sara?" asked Bart quietly.

"What I want?" Tears started flowing down her face as she looked into Bart's face. Bart was sorely tempted to reach out and brush the tears away with his fingertips, but he was frozen to his seat.

"It's what I **choose**, Bart." Then softly, "It's what I choose, Bart."

Turning around, Bart numbly slapped the reins starting the horse forward jerking the buggy into motion. Softly Bart said aloud, "I love you, Sara."

No sound came from the back of the buggy where the little lady continued to weep softly.

Half an hour later, Bart reached the ranch house and brought the buggy to a stop. He climbed down from his seat and helped a very subdued Sara from the buggy.

"Could you please carry the dishes up to the kitchen for me? You can leave them on the table and I'll tend to them later. And please tell Tennyson that I'm fine – I just needed to get off my feet and rest."

Sara turned and climbed the steps to the house and disappeared from sight. Bart complied with Sara's wishes, carrying the empty dishes and food up to the kitchen. She was nowhere to be seen. Bart returned to the buggy, and deftly turning the conveyance around, he went back to town.

CHAPTER FORTY-TWO

GOOD-BYE

Tennyson saw Bart outside the livery where Bart had returned the buggy before going to see the fireworks. Bart was leading Sampson out for the ride home.

"Bart! Glad to see you made it back before the speeches were over. I saw your face in the crowd and it was a boost to my confidence. I only wish Sara could have been here for it. She's my number one cheering section. How was she doing when you got her home?"

"Better, Boss. She went into the house and disappeared while I carried up the food and dishes to the kitchen. She was pretty exhausted. She probably called it a night, sir."

"It's been a long day for her, no doubt. Did you have any problems going home?"

"No, sir. It was a very quiet ride back to the house."

"I tell you what, Bart. If you don't mind, tie your horse onto the buggy and sit with me on the ride home so we can talk. I feel a little exhausted myself after the speech I was asked to make."

"Sure, Boss. I'll go get the buggy and be glad to drive it back." Bart went back into the livery and soon brought the horse and buggy outside. He tied his horse to the back of the buggy, then climbed back in beside Tenn.

"Giddap!" He called to the horse as he slapped the reins and started homeward for the second time that evening. For the first few miles, Tennyson talked about the different speeches that had been given. Bart answered with grunts in the right places for he was doing a lot of thinking about his future. Then hesitatingly, Bart spoke up.

"Boss, I want you to know how much it has meant to me that you were willing to take on a green boy and train him how to ranch and to act like a man. I will never forget the years I have spent at Keye Ranch."

"Sounds like you're fixing to leave us, Bart. Is there something wrong?"

"No, nothing is wrong. It's just that I want to start my own ranch somewhere and I don't want to be an old man when I do it."

Tennyson chuckled, "I think you're safe from being an old man for quite a few years. Seems to me, there's another reason you want to go. Am I right, boy?"

"Well, yes, maybe. I just feel like I need to move on or I'll bust wide open."

"Bust wide open, eh? That takes a lot of emotions to feel that way. It wouldn't be about

GOOD-BYE

a girl now, would it?" Tennyson watched Bart carefully. Bart kept his eyes straight ahead for he didn't dare look at Tenn.

"Maybe, but it is a useless situation and I feel like I ought to move on and be out of the way."

"I see." Tennyson was quiet for a few minutes before he spoke again. "Bart, could you stop the buggy for a few minutes, please?"

Bart pulled the buggy to a stop in practically the exact spot he had stopped with Sara.

"Thank you," said Tenn. "Now Bart, you've never been one to go into town to whoop it up on the week-ends, and I've never seen you talk to another girl at church, so I'm thinking this problem is a lot closer to home." Tennyson waited for Bart.

Bart was trapped. He should have known that Tennyson would see right through him, he always could. How could he tell the man that has been like a father to him that he loved his wife? Bart gave Tennyson a miserable look, and then turned to stare at the horse in front of him.

Quietly, Tennyson spoke up. "It's Sara, isn't it?"

Bart hung his head. How much he wanted to cry, but he couldn't give in to his feelings. He had to go, he had to leave.

"Boss, I want you to know that the only thing we've ever exchanged has been a few words. There has never been, and never will be anything between us. Of that, you can be assured."

Tennyson spoke as though he never heard Bart's words. "It was the dance tonight, wasn't it? The waltz can certainly cause a man to lose his heart. Unfortunately, I threw her into your arms. But Bart, you would have realized how you felt whether you had danced with her or not. It was bound to happen sometime. Both of you are young. Love is a strong emotion when you are young."

"I am ashamed of myself, Boss; to love a married woman and pregnant to boot. What awful things you must think of me. I must be a real disappointment to you."

"Bart, when you reach my age, there are a lot of things you understand. One of those things is love. You see, Bart, I love Sara and I know Sara loves me, but neither of us are in love with the other. Before we were married, I told Sara that she would be falling in love with someone soon, and was she sure she wanted to be married. Well, you know Sara. Did she admit she loved you, too?

"She said she had married her hero and an honorable man. There was nothing she would do to hurt him or dishonor his name. She was married to him until death parted them and that was that."

"Sounds like my Sara," grinned Tenn. "For a young girl, she has a lot of spit and fire in her. I found that even I with all the wisdom of my

GOOD-BYE

years couldn't stand against her spirit. I don't try to, it's a useless gesture."

"That's why I can't stay, Boss. It would be torture to be so close and yet, so far away."

"Well, Bart, let me ask you one thing. If you knew that within a year, Sara would be a widow, free and clear of her vows, could you wait for her?"

"Boss, what are you saying? You've got plenty of years ahead of you. And what about the baby – you want to see your child grow up, don't you?" Bart looked into Tennyson's face and what he saw there was hopelessness.

"I do, Bart, I do, but I won't. Doc says my heart is weakening quickly. I'll be lucky to see Sara deliver the baby. By the way, it's going to be a girl, Arabella Lacy. The good Lord told me that. Bart, you need to stay on for Sara's sake. She'll be lost. I've tried to make some provision for her, but she is going to need love to carry her through. Ned wants to come back and run the ranch and I'm proud he wants to do so. But I know my Sara. She'll leave the day after I'm buried. Don't let her leave alone."

Bart did have tears in his eyes now. Keye Ranch without Tennyson would never be the same.

"Boss, are you sure this doctor has it right? Maybe someone else will say something different."

Tennyson patted Bart's knee with his hand. "It's going to be fine. You see, I'll be home with Carolyn, and she is the one I love, besides my

Lord and Savior. You just rest easy and bide your time, son. It will be worth it all in the long run. Now I'm getting a bit tired, let's get on home."

Bart started the horse into action and continued on his way to Keye Ranch.

CHAPTER FORTY-THREE
DOCTOR

Tennyson was quiet as he entered the bedroom. Sara was fast asleep. He tiptoed over to her side and placed a kiss on her forehead.

Sleepily, Sara muttered, "Tennyson?"

"It's alright, Sara. The speech went fine. I'm so tired, I'm going to sleep. We'll talk in the morning." She murmured something unintelligible and was back asleep.

As Tennyson stepped back to go to his side of the bed, he kicked something soft. It was one of Sara's moccasins. He grinned as he remembered how she preferred them to tight fitting shoes. *Thank you, Lord, for this special lady in my life. I pray for her and for Bart. I hope they find the happiness together that Carolyn and I had. I couldn't ask for better parents for my Arabella Lacy. And Lord, I'm ready whenever You are. Amen.*

After the Fourth, it was hot and dry right through August. Bart and Tenn were thankful that when the springs dried up, the streams and river that cut through his land, still provided water for his cattle. The herd was doing well, and the two men discussed cutting the herd down and taking part of them to market. They would fetch a good price this year, and Tenn was concerned about the size of the herd when Ned took over. A smaller herd plus the cattle he would bring from his ranch, would give him a good herd and there would be plenty of money to fall back on in case of a problem.

Tennyson often made trips to town without Sara. She said it was pure torture to ride in a bouncing buggy in her condition, let alone a buckboard. She would only do that for church. Tennyson was just as glad about it, as he made regular trips to see the doctor and the lawyer, to make sure all was in readiness when the time came. He also would go down and visit with the Judge and talk about what he wanted for his children and for Sara. The Judge said he had to admit, that Tennyson had picked a pretty wonderful girl for a wife, even if there were several decades between them.

At the end of August, the doctor suggested that Tennyson not make any more visits to see him. He would come out to the ranch. They agreed that this being the last month of Sara's pregnancy, they didn't have to make up excuses. The doctor would be out weekly, and Tennyson was to stay off his horse if at all possible.

"You know, Mr. Keye, I only say that because we're trying to keep you alive so you can see this baby girl you insist Sara is having. You must have a better route to the Lord than I do, because I never know a baby's gender this side of delivery."

Before canning time came, Tenn had found a woman who was willing to help Sara with the work. Mahala picked and cleaned and stood over the hot stove while Sara measured and followed her recipes. The two ladies worked well together, and Tennyson paid Mahala a good wage for her work. Mahala took care of cleaning the house as well.

When the canning season was over, Sara found she had just enough energy to get up, dress and crochet or rest. Her feet stayed swollen and her toes look like sausages. She often wondered if she would ever have normal feet again. She thanked the good Lord daily for her moccasins. She was convinced that she was going to have a litter, and not just one. Tennyson laughed and said there would only be one, and how proud he was of her.

One late night, when neither one seemed able to sleep, Sara asked Tennyson about their first one. She reminded him that they never got back to put a stone on his grave.

"There will be a stone, Sara, I promised. I aim to keep that promise."

Sara had noticed that Tennyson didn't go to town anymore and stayed close by in the house. She figured that it was her time drawing near that confined him and didn't suspect his pallor was from more than just being indoors. Bart checked in with the boss daily, and except for a greeting or tipping his hat her direction, he didn't seek her out to chat. Her heart longed for him, but she squelched any feelings down inside of her and fussed over Tennyson.

September rains cooled the air and Sara spent time out on the porch a lot. She loved the hills and mountains in the distance and often wished she knew how to paint the beautiful scenery before her.

Tennyson had taken on a nagging cough that he didn't seem to be able to get rid of no matter what she tried. When the doctor came to check her, she asked him to check on Tennyson, which he did. He said that everything was as good as could be expected and not to worry about the coughing. It would end soon enough.

Sara kept the doctor's words in her mind's eye and kept playing them over and over again. She knew the coughing *was* something to worry about, but what did he mean it would end soon enough? Sara prayed to her Lord for understanding and when she got a glimpse at what it could mean, she was sorry to know.

She looked at Tennyson with new eyes and could see for herself that he had gone downhill in his health. There was a gray pallor in his face and the coughing was soon joined by some wheezing. She had to talk with someone about this. She didn't want to mention it to Tennyson. So she searched out Bart.

"Bart, could I speak with you for a moment, please?" she asked when she found him in the barn working with some of the other hands.

"Certainly, Miss Sara, how can I help you?"

She told Bart all she had noticed. She talked to him about the doctor's words, and how he said the coughing would soon come to an end. She told him what she suspected.

"Tennyson's dying, isn't he? Tell me the truth, Bart. I couldn't bear to be lied to right now." Sara's eyes pleaded.

Bart looked down into her eyes, and knew the words he would speak to her would break her heart. But he would not lie to Sara, not ever. As he told her what he knew, she broke down and wept in his arms. He simply held her. There was nothing else he could do to comfort her.

When she finally pulled herself together, she asked Bart how soon.

"He's hoping to see the baby born."

With tears in her eyes, she nodded. She turned and went back to the house.

CHAPTER FORTY-FOUR

PARTING

The hardest thing Sara ever tried to do was to pretend with Tennyson that there was nothing wrong. Tennyson allowed her pretending go on a couple of days, and then one evening he talked with her.

"Sara, you've been pussy-footing around me for the last three days. I don't know how you know, but obviously you do. Let's not pretend. Our time together is too precious to be spent in facades and pretending."

Sara looked at her hero with tears in her eyes and said, "Oh Tennyson. How can I go on without you? I know you'll be in a better place with Carolyn, but I'm so selfish, I need you here." She leaned against his shoulder and let the tears fall. Tennyson patted her and spoke soothing words to her.

"Sara, you're going to be all right. I've spoken to our heavenly Father and He has plans for good for you and you can rejoice in them."

"I don't know if I'll ever be able to rejoice again about anything."

"Now Sara, of course you will. You have your joy in the Lord and no one can take that from you. You'll have a wonderful life with our newborn baby and no one can take her from you."

"You think she is a girl, don't you Tennyson?" asked Sara.

"I *know* so. Arabella Lacy Keye. She'll be tiny and dainty like her mother and have her father's infectious smile." He grinned making Sara smile.

"Oh Tennyson, it has been so wonderful being with you. I am so honored to be your wife, even if it wasn't a love match."

"I don't know about that, Sara. I have such a special love for you, unlike any other. And because I'm not a young buck, I don't give my love away frivolously or on the spur of the moment. I've been blessed by the Almighty Himself in having you for a wife. From ice maiden to spit fire, you certainly have swept this old codger off his feet."

"There was no sweeping done. For heroism above and beyond the call of duty is what you have done for me. Tennyson, you will always be my hero, and I will make sure your daughter knows all about her special father." Sara laid her head on his shoulder and they each sat there in perfect silence, glad to be there before the fire, safe in their love.

They went to bed early that night. Two hours later, Sara awoke to the terrible coughing Tennyson was doing. She found extra pillows and tried to get him to sit up which seemed to help him breathe better.

"Thank you, dear. That is much better." Tennyson weakly whispered to her.

As Sara lay back down on her side of the bed, she felt a low cramp on her one side. It abated and she was able to relax. But by morning, she knew she was in labor and Tennyson had grown much weaker during the night. She made it to the doorway of the stairs and called to Mahala to tell one of the ranch hands to get the doctor double quick. She was in labor and Tennyson was dying.

Sara had made the room ready across the hall to have her baby. She didn't want to disturb Tennyson and knew she must not call out and worry him. She had kissed him and told him she was in labor and he said not to worry. The labor would not be long. How he knew, she didn't know. By one o'clock in the afternoon, a healthy baby girl was delivered and Sara felt the bittersweet mixture of love and grief. After resting for an hour or so, with Mahala's help and against the advice of the doctor, Sara walked across the hall so Tennyson could hold his baby daughter.

He looked upon her with such love and kissed her on top of her head like he always did her mama. "You've done me proud, little wife. You've done me proud." He handed her back to Sara when a fit of coughing took hold of him. Sara handed the baby to Mahala and wrapped her arms around Tennyson with soothing words and verses to comfort him.

At four o'clock the same afternoon, Tennyson passed from this world into the next. Sara was there as she had promised and with her tiny hands, closed the lids of the most loving eyes she had ever seen. She felt overwhelmed with grief, but refused to let the grief have control. There were things that had to be done and she wanted them done right. With moist eyes, she kissed Tennyson for the last time.

"Good-bye, Tennyson, my husband. Good-bye, my hero."

CHAPTER FORTY-FIVE

DETAILS

As soon as Tenn's body was ready, Bart brought the wagon around. They put the body in the back and covered it with a piece of canvas. Bart slowly climbed up and started into town.

It was a long ride for Bart. Tenn had been a role model for him for so long, almost a father figure. Bart thought about Sara and how much he ached for her as she cared so much for Tennyson. She had remained faithful to him to the very end. Bart stopped at the place along the road where he had stopped with both Sara and Tennyson on last Fourth of July.

Well, Boss, it hardly seems like three months ago we stopped here and talked. I promise you, whether or not we marry, I will look out for Sara. I'll run her ranch for her and see that she has what she needs. Thanks to you, she should do fine and your little daughter should be fine as well. Thank you, Boss, for being willing to put up with an overgrown scrawny boy who didn't know much. You are the reason I'm the man I am today.

Bart started the team up again and continued on into town. He went straight to the undertaker's and left the wagon there. He walked over to the depot and sent out two telegrams to Tenn's children. He walked over to the lawyer's office, and though he was closed for the day, Bart knocked long and hard, for the lawyer lived upstairs above the office. When the door was answered, Bart spoke with him for a few minutes and then left. His last stop was near the end of the street at the Judge's house. Judge Lawson came out to the porch and sat there talking with Bart about the day's events. Judge said he remembered Tennyson when he first came to Bloomfield.

"He wasn't much older than you were when you came here, Bart. I remember he was green, but had a lot of guts. Old man Guthrie owned the ranch then. He never had any children, but he took a liking to Tennyson and took him under his wing. Tennyson worked for him for fifteen years. Then Guthrie had a stoke and died leaving the ranch to him. Guthrie had no one else to leave it to, except the young boy he had taken under his wing, who had now become his foreman. Of course, Guthrie's acreage was a fourth of what Keye Ranch is today. Tennyson worked hard to build it up, he and Carolyn."

Bart asked, "Was he married when Guthrie died?"

"Oh my, yes. He was about 21 when he met Carolyn. She was the daughter of our new preacher. Tennyson had his hands full in courting that one. She gave him a lot of grief until the Sunday that he walked the aisle and accepted Christ as his Lord and Savior. After that, he had the inside track on the other young men. Now don't get me wrong, his conversion was real. So was his love for Carolyn. They had a wonderful life together. When she passed away, I thought Tennyson would never recover and from what he told me, he wouldn't have if he hadn't found Sara. He was contemplating ending his life at the mountain cabin when he found her. Taking care of Sara gave him a reason to go on living."

"I wondered at the time why he wanted to go and stay at that cabin. I didn't realize how bad he was feeling," Bart admitted. "I knew he had lost interest in the ranch and was leaving more and more decisions up to me."

"I didn't know either until he came and talked to me about marrying this young girl. I opposed the marriage from the beginning. I used every argument in the book trying to talk him out of it. But he wouldn't budge, and told me he knew what he was doing – that the Lord was behind it. I know when I met Sara and saw how young she was, I gave Tennyson such a look. Sara caught it and told me then that she would be the best wife she knew how to be for Tennyson and would honor her vows. That she certainly has done."

They talked a few more minutes as the darkness settled in around them. Shaking hands with Judge Lawson, Bart stepped down from the porch and walked back into town. He thought about Tenn as a young man taken in by Guthrie. Tenn had more or less followed his mentor's footsteps by taking Bart under his wing.

Bart stopped by for the wagon and team and drove them back to the ranch. It had been a long day and he was bone tired. He could have stayed in town for the night, but he was anxious to check on Sara and the baby. He began praying, asking for the Lord's guidance and direction as well as strength to get through the next few days.

After Sara said her final good-bye to Tennyson, Mahala helped her back into bed. Sara wasn't sure what she would have done without her the last few months. Mahala had taken care of washing and dressing Tennyson, before they took him to town. She tended the baby and brought her to Sara when she needed feeding.

Sara's heart felt so heavy. She had lost the best friend she had ever had, but she was so thankful she had known him. Her hero, her friend, and the father of her little one was certainly deserving of the rest he now had in heaven.

Sara closed her eyes. There was so many things to do, to think about before the funeral.

Mahala told her she would take care of everything at the house. Sara still needed to . . . she drifted off into a well deserved, though troubled sleep. She never knew that a tall worried cowboy just arrived back from town and was checking in with Mahala to see how the missus and the baby were doing.

Mahala woke Sara up for each of Arabella Lacy's feedings. Sara was so tired, that she immediately fell back to sleep. It wasn't until mid-morning that she woke up and stayed awake. She carefully made her way downstairs to the kitchen where Mahala scolded her for being out of bed.

"Mahala, if I don't start doing right now, I'll never make it through the funeral," said Sara.

"You don't need to go to the funeral. You have a newborn baby that needs you close at hand. You would be gone for hours. You cannot go. Everyone will understand," insisted Mahala.

"Maybe so, but I won't understand. I am going to be there. Even if I have to take Arabella Lacy with me." Sara was insistent.

"That baby is too little for you to be taking her to a funeral. What kind of mother would do that, I ask?"

"One who dearly loved and cared about the baby's father. I understand what you are saying, Mahala, but there must be a way. What if I get a room at the hotel for the day? I could feed the baby before the funeral and leave her there with you to watch her. When the funeral is over, I'll return to the hotel where

I can rest and feed her again before we head out for home."

"I don't know. It might work. I still don't like taking the baby out." Mahala wrinkled her brow as she spoke.

"It's Indian summer right now and the weather is not cold. The baby will be fine, especially with you there to care for her. Will you do it, Mahala?"

"I will do it," she said reluctantly.

When Bart checked in that morning before leaving to go into town, he was told of the plans that Sara had for the day of the funeral.

"I need you to reserve a room for me at the hotel for the day of the funeral, Bart."

"I don't think that is a good idea. This is only your first full day since you had the baby. Both of you ought to stay here and rest. Everyone will understand and won't be surprised that you aren't there."

Sara was dead set on her plan. Bart couldn't talk her out of it, so he agreed to check about a hotel room. He asked if there was anything else she needed from town as he was heading in to see if there was any news from Ned or Josie. If there was, he could go ahead and set up arrangements for the funeral.

"Just one more thing, Bart. I need you to go to the millinery shop and tell them I'll need a large brim hat with a mourning veil."

Bart made a slight face, but Sara said he wasn't the first man to ever enter a hat shop and survive. He didn't have to try it on after all. Bart shook his head and made good his escape through the kitchen door.

Sampson stood outside, saddled and waiting for Bart's return. Bart mounted and they left for town. Once there, Bart stopped at the train depot for any telegrams. There was one waiting for him. Ned was due in on the late afternoon train, but said he would rent a buggy from the livery to make it out to the ranch. His wife had just delivered a nine pound baby boy they named Jackson and she wasn't able to travel. Josie was due any day now, so she nor her husband would be able to come.

Next Bart stopped in to speak with the undertaker, then he went to see the pastor of the church. Once the funeral arrangements were made, he visited the lawyer and Judge Lawson to keep them informed of what was happening. They would bury Tennyson on Friday at ten o'clock in the morning. Today was Wednesday, and Ned would be there by evening. Bart also stopped at the hotel and made a room reservation for Friday. That left him with one more stop to make at the millinery shop to order the hat and veil for Sara. Bart would be glad to get that over with and head back to the ranch.

At home, Sara was trying on her black dress. It was the one she was wearing the day Tennyson found her. The dress definitely needed letting out in some of the seams, but she and Mahala thought they could do the alterations. *I know what you would say, Tennyson. I should go buy another dress. Well, I refuse to buy a new black dress when I already have one that is serviceable. It's a waste of good money on a dress that is such an ugly color. But I will get a new hat and veil. Remember how I lost the other one? It was the veil that lead you to me. Now it will be another veil that will part you from me. I miss you so much, Tennyson.* Sara let the tears cleanse her heart of the loss she felt.

Ned arrived that evening. He shared the news that he was the father of a strapping boy, and that Josie was waiting on hers to arrive at any time. He admired his half-sister and asked Sara how they were getting along. They talked about Tennyson and Ned shared some memories he had of growing up with his dad.

The next morning Ned left to go over the ranch with Bart and talk. Sara and Mahala worked on her dress alterations, then Mahala pressed it and had it ready for the next day. The day seemed to drag on, but Sara rested as much as she could knowing that the next day would be long and tiring. Several neighbors stopped in to share their condolences and provide some food, all of which Sara graciously thanked them for their care and concern.

She also received a note from J.W. Drew, Attorney at Law, stating that he would like to meet with Ned and Sara at the ranch at ten o'clock Saturday morning to go over Tennyson's will. Sara didn't expect anything as she had told Tennyson she wouldn't take anything from his children's inheritance. Maybe there was something for Lacy in his will. Sara was thinking of her more and more as Lacy since Arabella Lacy was such a long name for such a little girl. Tennyson was always thinking of others. Bart also was suppose to be present.

Sara knew she needed to start making plans for herself and Lacy. They would need to make a home in another town where she could find work. But what could she do? Sara's head ached at the thought, but she knew she couldn't make any decisions until after the funeral was past.

Eventually the day came to an end. Everyone turned in early. The house was quiet though soft weeping could be heard from Sara's room.

CHAPTER FORTY-SIX

FUNERAL

The next day was cloud covered and gloomy. Sara thought it reflected how she felt. They loaded the buggy with her baggage as well as Lacy's with Mahala sitting in the back with the baby where there was the most protection from the elements. Sara rode beside Bart and Ned followed in his buggy. The trip was a quiet one and Bart drove them straight to the hotel to allow Sara, Lacy and Mahala to settle in and for Sara to change for the funeral. He went over to the hat shop and picked up Sara's order and delivered it to the hotel as well.

As the men checked on everything, Sara had time to feed Lacy and change clothes, without being rushed. Lacy was fast asleep in her makeshift crib when Sara put on her altered black dress. The hat was a large brim, but the sweeping veil covered her down to her waist. As Sara looked into the mirror, she thought of the other time she wore widow weeds to escape detection from Jud. Now she wore them for real to escape detection from onlookers. Her grief was a private thing, or so she felt.

When Sara came down the stairs to meet Bart, he didn't recognize her. The black dress and veil of course told him it was Sara, but she wore them with the maturity of an older woman in mourning, not a young girl whose whole life lay ahead of her. Bart offered his arm and escorted her out to the buggy and helped her settle in the back. The skies overhead looked ominous, but so far, there had been no rain.

The service at the church was packed. Tennyson had made so many friends in Bloomfield and everyone wanted to show their respect. Tennyson's young widow didn't make a sound as she sat with Ned and Bart throughout the service. When they loaded the coffin in the hearse, Sara stood and shook hands and nodded her head as sympathy and condolences were extended to her. At last, the cavalcade led the way out of town and up the hill to where the cemetery was. As everyone gathered around the grave, Sara stoically remained standing as the pastor committed Tennyson's body to the earth and his spirit to heaven.

At the last "Amen" the rain started. Just a sprinkle at first, but enough that many headed for their carriages. The pastor spoke a few words to Ned and Sara and then he, too, left for shelter. Ned stood for a few moments, then told Sara he would meet her back at the

FUNERAL

ranch. The grave diggers asked permission to start filling in the grave and Sara gave a single nod. As soon as they finished, they left as well. As the rain started in earnest, Bart and Sara were left at the graveside. Then Bart walked away leaving Sara. He knew it would be of no use to encourage her to leave. She would leave when she was ready.

Sara stood there alone. The drops of rain somehow seemed appropriate. She slowly removed her hat and veil and laid them on the grave before her. Tennyson would have appreciated the gesture, she thought. She fell to her knees with her head bowed and wept until the sobs slowed and stopped. Another stood close by waiting at the gate of the cemetery. He, too, had removed his hat, and like Sara, the tears also flowed on the face of the tall cowboy whose heart wept not only for his boss, but for the wife who kneeled at his grave. The rain continued until it, too, was played out and finally stopped. Then the two figures left the cemetery and headed back to the hotel.

CHAPTER FORTY-SEVEN

INHERITANCE

*S*aturday dawned bright with sunshine and clear skies. Sara felt drained, but now that the funeral was behind her, she felt that she was ready to face what tomorrow would bring.

The lawyer and the judge were due at ten o'clock. Ned was supposed to catch the late afternoon train for home. Sara got up and dressed after feeding Lacy. Her time with Lacy in her arms gave her such a deep peace. *A peace that God gives to mothers no doubt,* thought Sara.

She went down to the kitchen and Mahala had breakfast waiting for her. For the first time in days, Sara was hungry and enjoyed the meal. She went into the study and did some Bible reading and prayed for the meeting ahead. *Father, I don't know what You have in store for Lacy and me, but we'll trust in You to provide as You always have. Thank you for the blessings you have given us in this home. Knowing what You have done in the past, gives me confidence that You will provide for the future. Whatever that future is, O Lord, I pray it is according to Your will. Amen.*

At ten o'clock, J.W. Drew and Judge Lawson arrived in a buggy. Lawyer Drew had a briefcase with him and looked so official. Judge Lawson came with an easy smile and an attitude everything would come out well.

They sat around the big dining room table, so the lawyer could spread out his papers and everyone could enjoy some of Mahala's coffee.

The will was pretty straight forward. The contents were read by Mr. Drew in a very matter of fact manner without any comment.

First of all, Tennyson left a certain amount to the church to be used however they would see fit to use it. However, he wanted no labels or dedications made in his name. He was simply giving back to the Lord, a portion of what the Lord had given him.

Ned was to inherit the estate known as Keye Ranch with the house, outbuildings, acreage, and all stock associated with it. It was Tennyson's hope that Ned would be successful in ranching and leave it as an inheritance to his son.

Josie was to inherit a goodly sum of money to be transferred to a bank of her choice. It would be set up as a trust fund with a large amount that she could draw on each year.

Bart, who had served him faithfully and had kept the ranch from failing the last two years, was to receive a specified amount of cash to do with as he willed. (Bart gave a low whistle at the amount. He never dreamed how much Tennyson was worth.)

The lawyer finally read the last section of the will. "Last of all, to my wife, Sara Morrow Keye, who has faithfully honored her vows, given me a reason for living, and has born me my final child, I bequeath a small estate in the mountains which also has a barn and attached cabin to be hers in trust, to do with as she sees fit, until our daughter reaches maturity. A trust fund has also been set up for her in the Bloomfield Bank on which she may draw a sum of money each year for the remainder of her life or the funds are depleted. To my daughter, Arabella Lacy, I give the mountain home and lands to her upon reaching the age of twenty-five. I also want my wife, Sara, to please note that this purchase of property was made after the death of my first wife, Carolyn, and with money that did not come out of the estate known as Keye Ranch. Instead it came from my mentor, Amos Guthrie, who left it to me to use however I would choose. As promised to my wife, none of the inheritance from the Keye Ranch would be given to her, but only to my two adult children."

The will concluded with the words, "May the Keye name continue to bring honor to those who bear it." Mr. Drew came to a close by putting the will down on the table, removing his spectacles and asking if there were questions.

Ned seemed pleased and voiced that he was sure his sister would be pleased as well. Bart said he was dumbfounded by his boss's generosity. He had given Bart so much already by taking him in and teaching him how to run a successful ranch.

All eyes then turned to Sara. She sat there with a very small smile on her face and had turned deathly pale. At last, she spoke, "I'm glad Tennyson included the part of where the inheritance for me and Lacy came from, for he knew I would not accept it if it was taken from Ned or Josie's. I never dreamed he had so much when I married him."

Following this, Judge Lawson spoke up to address the group.

"I've known Tennyson since we were both young enough to dream and old enough to work. He has been a straight arrow from the start and I couldn't have asked for a better friend. When he was planning what to put in his final will, he came to me. Several times, in fact, for the one thing he wanted more than anything else, is that his will would not cause any breach in the family. He asked me to be here to make sure that did not happen. I can see now, that it hasn't and I don't believe it will. The problem with having the almighty dollar is knowing how to live without letting it overtake you and run your life. Tennyson knew that and lived by it.

"Ned, your father was so proud of the man you have become, especially when he knew he wasn't always there for you as much as he wanted to be. He wanted Josie to have the freedom and finances to build a good life with her husband and provide for her children.

"Bart, he thought of you as a younger version of himself. You have not only done all he could have asked for, but you were instrumental in saving the herd these past winters by your own ingenuity. He wanted you to have the additional funds to do as you would like. He spoke that you dreamed of your own place and he wanted you to be able to make that dream come true. Just as Guthrie left him a sum to invest or spend, he wanted to do the same for you.

"Sara, I can't tell you how wrong I was about you that first day I met you, nor how right Tennyson was about marrying you. You gave him room to remember yesterday, a reason for today and hope for tomorrow. He didn't want to leave you this soon, but he said the Lord had other plans for you and for him. Plans for good and for an abundant life. He asked me to tell you to go back to the cabin and raise Arabella Lacy in the mountains you love. And he said, 'Tell Sara, I was honored to be her hero and her husband.' He also told me that you would know what that meant."

Sara suddenly stood up and quickly walked out of the room and into the kitchen. The ones at the table heard the back door open and close. The Judge broke the silence by clearing his voice.

"Now everyone, I must get back to town, unless there are questions?" He looked at Ned and Bart who shook their heads.

"No? Very well, then, J.W. and I will be on our way. Good day to you all." With that, he stood and he and Mr. Drew left for town.

As soon as the Judge and lawyer were gone, Bart started looking for Sara. At first he didn't see her, but he heard a soft cry in the distance. He found her down by the cattle barn weeping her heart out. A couple of the hands were watching her with concern on their faces. As soon as they spotted Bart, they nodded their heads and disappeared. He came up to her and wrapped his arms around her and let her cry.

"I'm sorry I left so abruptly. I don't know what came over me, or why I'm crying." Sara choked the words out between sobs.

"There now, Sara. It's all the emotion that you've been carrying around while you put up a brave front. You loved Tennyson and you have a big hole in your life now he is gone. I do, too. It will take time for us to grieve for his loss. You will come to your old self again. It won't happen overnight, but you will. For now, let the tears flow when they come and they will help you to heal."

Sara finally stopped weeping, and outside of an occasional hiccough, she quieted down in Bart's arms. She looked up into his blue eyes.

"And what about us Bart? Are you sure you want to put up with me and Lacy?"

"I think I will answer that question next spring. For now, Sara, you need time to adjust to Tennyson's death and Lacy needs your undivided attention. When you come to yourself, and you will, we'll make plans for our future together. I'll be around until then."

"Thank you, Bart." Sara took a deep breath. "I suppose the Judge and Mr. Drew have headed back to town."

"Yes, they have. Mahala was getting ready to serve dinner. Let's head back to the house."

Mahala did indeed have the meal ready when they returned. Everyone sat in silence as they ate. Finally, Sara spoke up.

"What I don't understand about the will, is that it was written several months ago and the baby hadn't been born. How did Tennyson know that it would be a girl?"

Bart spoke up, "He shared with me that God told him it would be a girl and that he would see her. He never had any doubt about it."

"It's a good thing she was born a girl," exclaimed Ned, "since Dad named the child Arabella Lacy in the will. A boy with that name would find life pretty tough to live down otherwise!" Everyone smiled at Ned's comment. The silence was broken and the rest of the meal was shared in a lighter atmosphere.

After everyone had finished and Mahala began to clear the table, Sara slipped upstairs to tend to Lacy, while Bart and Ned went outside to talk more about the ranch until it was time for Ned to leave.

Sara went into the bedroom and picked up her daughter who stretched and yawned. Sara's heart was full. Tennyson was still caring for her from the other side of the grave. He would always be the hero she could never forget. Lacy started to cry needing her mother's attention, which Sara happily gave to her.

CHAPTER FORTY-EIGHT

HOME

Ten months later on an unusually Warm summer day, Sara sat out in front of the mountain cabin and watched as Lacy toddled around the yard. Sara smiled, as Lacy was certainly not going to be petite and dainty. She was more like a string bean and seemed to be fearless. Sara learned from the day that Lacy took her first step, that she had to be watched. The world was wide open to this toddler and she wasn't afraid to take it on.

Sara looked around at the cabin and the mountains. The cabin was hers! Sara still couldn't believe that Tennyson had given it to her. She also was amazed to find it had two hundred acres that went with it. Enough to ranch a little, farm a little, and make a good life. When Sara arrived at the cabin, she was saddened to think that she and Tennyson never made it back to the cabin together. Those months they spent together in the cabin would always be a special memory in her heart.

She had stayed that winter at the ranch. Ned didn't plan to move there until the spring, so he asked Sara to stay on with Lacy. Bart also agreed to stay until the spring, when he would resign as foreman of the Keye Ranch. He and Ned had talked, and Bart told him that Ned didn't need a foreman, as he was quite capable of running the ranch himself. Ned thanked him for staying at the ranch through the winter.

Bart and Sara spent the winter getting to know each other. Bart wanted Sara to have the time she needed to recover from losing Tennyson, but by March, Sara knew she was ready to go on with the life Tennyson wanted her to have. She and Bart planned a quiet May wedding.

Sara also got the opportunity to write to Betty and Flo and let them know all that had transpired. She only sent one letter, knowing they would share between them. Three weeks later she got an answer to her letter. Betty had had twins, a boy and a girl, and she and Henry were looking for a house. Flo's walk with the teacher the night Sara left, started a fire under the sheriff and he and Flo married that spring. She was expecting her first child this summer.

Finally the day came in May. Bart and Sara knocked on Judge Lawson's door and he once again married the couple before him with no doubts of their suitability for each other. After the ceremony, Sara and Bart moved into the cabin as Ned and his family were due at the ranch the middle of May.

The first day she arrived, she went to look at Mathias T Keye's grave. Sure enough, a granite marker had replaced the wooden cross Tennyson had fashioned. *You kept your promise, Tennyson, you kept it.*

Bart and Sara spent the summer getting the ranch into shape and enjoying Lacy. Sara shared with Bart the tunnels with the spring room and living room. Bart even discovered the secret back tunnel that Tennyson had used when the robbers had taken over. Soon the summer turned to fall. The months of October and November flew by as both Bart and Sara were happy in the love they had found in each other.

Sara sat up quickly from her reminiscing. Lacy was nowhere in sight. *Where could that girl have gone now?* A burst of giggles was heard off to her right and as she stepped that direction, a tall cowhand carrying a spindly little toddler on his shoulder came into view. Sara's heart swelled. *'Rejoice in the Lord alway, and again I say rejoice!' You were right, Tennyson, I do have a full and wondrous life to rejoice in and sing praises. Oh, Tennyson, you'll always be my hero, to love and honor all my days.*

This Christmas would be a second special Christmas in the cabin for Sara. She would also have to order another package of material and things to work on over the winter for the baby that would be arriving in the spring. She planned to tell Bart soon about the baby she was carrying. This time, however, she didn't have the morning sickness she had had before.

So much had happened to her in the last two and a half years. Looking back, Sara could see the plan God had for her life and how He had been with her each step of the way.

A cry of delight escaped from the toddler that was being carried on top of the shoulders of her papa. Sara walked over to the tall cowhand with the blue eyes and dark hair. She stood on her tiptoes and leaned against him to kiss him. Lacy giggled and they all laughed together in perfect harmony as they walked home arm in arm to the cabin in the mountains.

CPSIA information can be obtained
at www.ICGtesting.com
Printed in the USA
FFOW04n0924101015